THE INNOCENT WIFE

SALLY ROYER-DERR

Storm
PUBLISHING

This is a work of fiction. Names, characters, business, events and incidents are the products of the author's imagination. Any resemblance to actual persons, living or dead, or actual events is purely coincidental.

Copyright © Sally Royer-Derr, 2025

The moral right of the author has been asserted.

All rights reserved. No part of this book may be reproduced or used in any manner without the prior written permission of the copyright owner.

To request permissions, contact the publisher at rights@stormpublishing.co

Ebook ISBN: 978-1-80508-830-1
Paperback ISBN: 978-1-80508-832-5

Cover design: Sara Simpson
Cover images: Shutterstock

Published by Storm Publishing.
For further information, visit:
www.stormpublishing.co

ALSO BY SALLY ROYER-DERR

The Secrets Next Door

The Forever Home

Ohana

The Tracks

High Bluffs Trilogy

High Bluffs

Santa Monica

The Return

To my friends at Penn-Bernville Elementary School who kept telling me to write a story in a school setting, this one's for you! (yes, this book is entirely fictional)

PROLOGUE

I stand by the curtains in the bedroom watching the light fabric dance in the breeze flowing through the half-open window. The late September air is cool and crisp.

My lips are dry, and I lick them slowly, eyeing the glass of water sitting on the nightstand next to me. The ice is almost melted; just half a cube lingers. I lift the glass, hesitating to take a sip, his words repeating in my mind.

I throw the glass against the wall.

It breaks, shattering to the floor, splaying broken, jagged glass across the soft, carpeted surface. I've heard the definition of insanity is doing the same thing over and over again and expecting a different result. After all these years, maybe I should be committed.

But did I expect a different result? Or did I do the same thing over and over again to keep everything calm and unchanging?

To keep him happy.

I shiver and think of him again. Why do I allow him to consume my thoughts so much? Why do I give him such power?

I close my eyes and try to erase him from my memory, if only for a moment.

My hands shake and I try to still them, but the tremors only pause for a moment. I stare at them in the dim light—only a small lamp is on in the corner of the room. I haven't moisturized today, and my hands feel dry, my skin brittle and old.

Dried up.

Like me.

I look around the comfortable, tastefully decorated room. Of course it's tastefully decorated: I did it. Pretty, soft colors, plush bed, a sleek, gray wingback chair. My lair.

My fucking prison.

ONE

Natalie

I peer into the mirror above the bathroom sink and apply a touch of mascara to my eyelashes, then stand back to assess myself. My dark brunette hair, with a hint of reddish highlights, is newly cut into a sleek bob, my makeup is light and fresh, and a hint of a smile plays on my lips. Butterflies dancing in my stomach remind me a new adventure awaits me today.

"Mommy!" my five-year-old daughter, Emma, bursts into the bathroom. She's dressed in a pretty pink dress with a colorful rainbow decorating the front. She twirls around. "Look at me!"

"Oh, you look so pretty!" I exclaim.

"Will you put my ribbon in?" she asks, handing me a hair clip bursting with different colored ribbons that she insisted on buying at the mall last week. I sigh, trying to push away the butterflies wreaking havoc on my stomach. Today is her first day of kindergarten. She isn't nervous, but I am, not only for her but myself too. Today I start my new job at Peyton Heights East

Elementary as a learning support teacher for third and fourth grade.

I clip the ribbon into Emma's long, dark wavy hair, just like mine at that age. I pick her up and we look into the bathroom mirror together. Her sweet round face presses close to mine.

"How do we look?" I ask, smiling.

She smiles too, gleaming white baby teeth. She hasn't lost any yet, but I suspect it won't be long, as her right front tooth is a bit wobbly.

"Like princesses!" she exclaims, kissing my cheek. She wiggles out of my arms. "Hurry, Mommy, we have to go soon. To school!"

I smile at her excitement, give my hair a quick tidy and sigh again. What a busy couple of months. First the divorce finalized from Jake, then my old school cut the budget, which meant my job in the special education department was axed. I need a good job to support Emma and myself, so I was scrambling to find something. The limited positions available so close to the beginning of the school year were taken quickly and I thought I may have to look at schools located farther away, but hated to do that, preferring to live and work fairly close to Jake. It would make everything so much easier with our shared custody of Emma. After interviewing for various positions, I was starting to lose hope when I was lucky enough to get this teaching job, and thrilled to find this two-bedroom townhouse to rent right across from the school. I couldn't have asked for a better location.

Emma is still buzzing from her star role as flower girl this weekend at Jake's wedding. I'm happy for him and Candace, truly, but I'm not sad that chatter about school has finally overtaken talk of Emma's sparkly peach dress and shoes. She took her job seriously, and I was proud of my entire unconventional family as I watched her walk ahead of Candace down the aisle. There were a few odd looks of course, that the ex-wife was attending, and so happily at that, but though I love Jake, our marriage was never romantic, and I am delighted that he's found love now. Jake deserves it, and maybe one day I'll find it too, but it's a low priority at this point. Right now, I'm just glad the summer is over; it's been such a whirlwind of busyness. We're settled into our new house, and I'll get into my new job, and hopefully just have a calm, regular life after all the changes over the last few months.

"Mommy, let's go," Emma calls from the kitchen.

"I'm coming," I reply, flicking off the bathroom light. Let's get this day started.

The first day of school is always a blur. Most of the morning involving checking in with Mrs. Link's third-grade class. I have four students in her class and one girl, Anna, will need substantial support. I reviewed her Individualized Education Program last night and have an idea of what strategies I'll use to help her reach her goals. Reading is her most difficult subject, so direct instruction in my classroom will likely be best for her, with some regular ed inclusion at times. In math, my paraprofessional, Abby, will push in for class instruction and support her. I think with the additional support in the regular ed classroom Anna will do well, but there is always the possibility of pull out for small group instruction.

I need to work on Abby's daily schedule but want to wait until I've seen the fourth-grade class this afternoon, then I'll have a good feel of the needs of each student on my caseload.

It's one thing to read through IEPs, and to study the disability diagnosis of my students, but it's more important to get to know them and see what environment and method is going to work best for them to reach their education goals. I love how rewarding it is when I find the right balance for a student that encourages them to thrive and love learning. It's such a thrill and one of the main reasons I became a teacher.

My stomach rumbles. I need to get my lunch. I debate just eating at my desk, but I'll have to go get my lunch bag from the refrigerator in the faculty room anyway. I'm not shy exactly, but there is something daunting about being the new teacher. I guess I should be social and eat lunch down there, maybe make some new friends.

I rise from my neatly organized desk and walk across the classroom, pausing to adjust the bright yellow kid-sized sofa under my Hello Sunshine bulletin board, my theme for the classroom. I'm thankful that I had enough time during the teacher in-service days before the first day of school to organize my new classroom. I love the cheery yellows, whites, and light blues with a splash of pink. From my yellow and white polka dot rug to the wooden vase of yellow sunflowers made from LEGO blocks, a gift from one of my former students, and another bulletin board declaring *This Class Is Brilliant!* All the cheerfulness lends a brightness to the room and makes me happy every time I walk into the space. I hope my students feel the same.

I walk down the hall, gleaming for the first week of school. It won't last long; soon muddy sneakers will dirty the hallway, too many to clean right away, and random pieces of paper, lost homework papers turning up here and there. Even a random sock may appear, something you would think one would notice, but it only ends up in the lost and found box by the office. I turn left and enter the faculty room. A loud cackle of laughter explodes from the back of the room.

The area isn't large, a small counter with a coffee pot, toaster, a refrigerator at the end of the counter to the right. A copier sits to the left, with another long counter filled with paper, staplers, assorted pens, and a telephone. A round clock hangs on the wall above the copier. Spread throughout the room are four round tables with four chairs at each table. Every chair is full, except one. Daphne Link, the third-grade teacher I worked with this morning, spots me and beckons me over.

I snatch my lunch bag from the fridge and slide into the empty chair beside her. The two other women on the table are vaguely familiar. I probably met them at the mandatory in-service orientation at the high school the week before school started. I met so many people that day, even if they look familiar, I still don't remember their names.

"So, Natalie," Daphne says, taking a sip of her bottled water, "how's your first day going?"

"Pretty good," I reply, unzipping my lunch bag and taking out my turkey sandwich, granola bar and yogurt. It's a new one with bright purple and green flowers that Emma picked for me at the Vera Bradley outlet store when we were shopping last week. "Third grade with you this morning was great. I have some ideas I want to discuss with you about Anna later."

"Oh, great." Daphne takes a bite of her sandwich. "Where are you after lunch?"

"Fourth grade. Um... L. Hanson. I haven't met her yet," I say, tearing open my granola bar.

Daphne laughs. "You mean him." She points to the back table. "Actually, that's Mr. Hanson back there."

"Oh." I turn to look but can only see the back of a man's head. His dark hair is smartly cut, but I can't see anything else from this angle.

"Lucas!" Daphne calls out.

Lucas.

Lucas Hanson. My skin pricks. It can't be him. He turns, and I see his face.

It is him. I duck back to my food, trying to gain a moment's composure. This can't be happening.

"What, Daph?" he asks, walking up behind me.

I can smell his cologne, woodsy and masculine, so familiar to me. Are the others picking up on my tension? I take a quick breath, steel myself, and turn around to see him standing next to me. This close, I can see the changes that have come through the years; his dark hair now has a bit of salt and pepper mixed in, but his tall lean frame looks the same as ever, housed in a crisp white dress shirt with dark blue stripes, dark blue tie and gray dress pants. His brown eyes seek mine, kind and gentle.

Just like I remember.

At least in the beginning.

"Lucas," Daphne says, and she motions to me. "This is Natalie Amaryllis. She's the new learning support teacher."

Lucas smiles at me and sticks out his hand. "Nice to meet you, Natalie."

I return his smile, awkwardly, and shake his outstretched hand, then quickly drop my hand down. "Nice to meet you too."

"You'll be in my room this afternoon I think, for Dylan and Heather?" he asks in a friendly voice.

"Yes, and Sam," I reply. My hand shakes, and I quickly dig into my lunch bag, pretending to search for something, to keep it busy.

A gale of laughter rises from the back table.

"Lucas!" one of the women calls. "You're missing all the fun!"

He laughs good-naturedly. "Okay, Debbie." He looks at me. "I'll look forward to working with you, Natalie." He walks away to rejoin Debbie and the other women at the back table.

"Oh, fourth grade likes to laugh," Daphne remarks, popping a grape into her mouth.

"I'd laugh at whatever Lucas told me," Lucy whispers, pushing her glasses up the bridge of her nose.

Everyone laughs. Daphne lowers her voice. "Yes, Lucy,

we're aware of your feelings about Lucas. You do know he's married."

"But still such a flirt," Lucy says. "Hey, it's all in good fun."

The women laugh again, and I murmur that I must make a phone call, gather my uneaten lunch, and scurry out the door.

TWO

Natalie

I race down the hall and run into my classroom. Sweat runs down my back and my hands continue to tremble. The classroom door slams shut, and the room is silent. Safe. I toss my lunch bag on the desk and pace the room.

Lucas Hanson.

Lucas Hanson.

For so many months he had been all I thought of, fantasized about, and tried to impress. I always thought he was movie-star handsome with his dark hair and eyes, chiseled chin and athletic build. Those attributes haven't changed. Even the dusting of silver in his hair only makes him more distinguished.

Thankfully, there's no way he recognized me. I haven't seen him in twenty years, not since I was fifteen. I look different, of course, probably a good twenty pounds heavier, my long hair is now in a short bob, not to mention my glasses and general aging. I'm not a girl anymore. He knew me when I was a girl.

When I was fifteen.

He was twenty-five.

And my soccer coach.

I collect my emotions during the last fifteen minutes of my lunch and by the time Abby, my paraprofessional, returns to the room, my nerves are not necessarily calm, but managed. Lucas didn't recognize me; our history can remain a dusty memory from the past. I need this job for me and Emma. No need to dig up the past and all its messiness. It was wrong on so many levels, but I will not dwell on it now. I have a job to do.

"How was second grade?" I ask her. Abby is with me for most of the day, but before her lunch she goes into second grade to assist with science.

"Pretty good. It's the first day; everybody is just reviewing the rules and talking about what's coming up," Abby replies, sitting her flowered bag on the back table. "After twenty-five years here, I could give the first day speeches myself."

I smile. "I'm sure you could. Well, I'm going to Mr. Hanson's class for math. I'll be back around one thirty."

"Oh, Lucas the ladies' man." Abby raises her eyebrows.

I force a laugh. "He does seem popular."

"He just likes to joke with everyone. You should see his wife," she replies.

"Really, why?"

"She's very pretty and *very* young," Abby says, picking up her flowered bag again. "Well, I'm off to lunch."

"Enjoy," I reply.

I'll bet she's young.

Curiosity nips at me. I glance at the clock. I must get moving.

I exit my classroom and walk slowly down the hall to the fourth-grade hallway. I nod to Daphne, who is leading her class from the library. I pause outside of Lucas's door and take a deep breath. I steel myself and go inside his classroom. I need this job.

"We'll be reviewing decimals and fractions tomorrow," he is saying to the class as I enter the room.

He turns and smiles at me. "Ah, class, this is Mrs. Amaryllis. She'll be joining us for math in the afternoon and sometimes pulling students to work in her classroom."

"Thank you, Mr. Hanson," I reply, nodding to the class. "I'm excited to be working with you all."

Another megawatt smile from him and he continues to talk about his math review tomorrow. "We're going to go over everything together and see what you remember from third grade. I always like to have a review to refresh our minds at the beginning of the school year."

I walk around to the back of the classroom, subtly noting where my students sit. One of them, Dylan, gnaws at his pencil so intensely as Mr. Hanson speaks, I fear he'll swallow some shards of wood. I whisper to him to put the pencil on the desk, which he does, thankfully.

I listen to Lucas speak, feeling a curious detachment spreading through myself. While my face and demeanor are professional and calm, my mind is a sea of turbulent emotions. I never thought I'd see him again. It never even crossed my mind. Jake and I grew up and went to a school about forty-five minutes away from here, and I've not been back for decades. That's where I had left Lucas in my mind. I still remember being on the soccer field with my team when he arrived. We'd been told we were getting a new coach, and all the girls were whispering about who it would be, gossiping and giggling as fourteen-year-olds do. When Lucas walked across the field in dark aviator sunglasses the chatter stilled.

It seems a lifetime ago and so incomprehensible to be standing in his classroom now. He taught sixth grade back then, and it was his first year as a high school soccer coach. I remember how eager he was to be coaching our team and developing our skills on the field.

And off the field too, but that came later.

To be fair to him, he was a good coach, a skilled athlete who had played soccer in high school and college. He was friendly, helpful, and kind. All the girls liked him. All the girls had a crush on him. All the girls wanted his attention, and I was no exception.

But he was a wolf in sheep's clothing. Most predators are, even though I didn't see it that way at the time. I was fifteen when we started our relationship. I didn't know any better. He was this incredibly good-looking guy, and he was interested in *me*! I could barely believe it. He was my first boyfriend, which is how I thought of him at the time. What did I know? I was a girl, and he was a man. He should have had boundaries with me. Things never should have gone as far as they did. He knew better, at least he should have.

"Mrs. Amaryllis?" Mr. Hanson's voice breaks into my thoughts. I look around; the students are now lined up at the door.

"Um... yes?" I stutter.

"We're going down to the welcome back assembly in the gym. Will you be joining us?"

I smile. "Of course, I'll be down in a few minutes. I have a quick stop to make."

"Great," he replies. "Okay, class, remember, quiet in the hallway."

After the last student leaves the classroom, I speed down to the faculty bathroom and sit in there a few minutes to clear my head. Seeing Lucas today sent my emotions reeling; I hadn't thought of him in years, but the sight of him today put me right back into those turbulent feelings of a fifteen-year-old, and when I think of how it all ended... my stomach retches.

. . .

"My new friend Becky wore a pink dress today. Just like me!" Emma exclaims. "It had white flowers on it."

"Oh, that's nice," I murmur, tossing her backpack and my bag into the backseat of my car.

"Becky's a walker. She walks to school with her older sister," Emma continues. "Can I wait at the walker door with Becky after school? She said she'll wait with me until you get me."

"I thought you wanted to wait in my classroom until I was finished with bus duty."

"No, I want to wait with Becky," she insists.

"Oh, okay, that's fine. Mrs. Stamos is at the walker door," I reply. "I'll let her know you'll wait with Becky after school until I get there."

"Or if Daddy picks me up?"

"Sure," I reply. "Sometimes Daddy picks you up if I have a meeting."

"Or Candace?"

"Yes, sometimes Candace if Daddy can't come, but that's it. You don't go with anybody else," I say as she hops into the backseat and secures her seatbelt.

"I like Candace, she's nice." Emma pouts. "But I wish Daddy still lived with us."

"I know things are different now, honey, but we love Daddy, and he loves us. Now our family is bigger because we have Candace too," I explain. I realize our situation is unusual. I think Emma realizes it too, in a way. Emma is smart; she sees the differences, sees that Jake and Candace share a bedroom while we always had separate rooms, but what is most important is that she knows she's loved by everyone.

"I love Daddy," she says softly. "And I love you and I like Candace."

I smile at my sweet daughter. "You're so funny."

She grins and accepts the juice box I give her. Grape juice, her favorite.

I get into the car, and we drive the short distance to our new home across the road from the school. Most days we'll walk to school too, but I had quite a few items to bring in today, so it made sense to drive. The road is busy at times and that is one constant worry in the back of my mind when Emma plays outside. Although our backyard is fenced, and Emma is good about following rules.

I hit the garage door opener and pull inside, hitting the button again to close the door behind me. We grab our bags and go inside the house. Emma runs upstairs, probably to play with her beloved Barbies, while I go to heat dinner. I made chicken alfredo yesterday, so we'll have those leftovers. I just need to steam some broccoli to go with it.

I toss my school bag and purse on the kitchen table and pick up Emma's backpack that she flung on the floor, hanging it on the chair. I peek inside the backpack to see the mountain of back-to-school paperwork I need to complete tonight.

I sigh, busying myself with preparing dinner, then open the fridge and pour an iced tea. What a day. Overall, everything went well but seeing Lucas was a punch in the gut that I can't seem to shake off. It was so many years ago, but I'll never forget about him. How could I, after everything that happened between us? I'm thankful he doesn't recognize me; that's the last thing I need.

At this point in my life my only concern is Emma, providing for her, giving her the best life I can. I thank God every day that we have Jake, even though things are different now, but he gave me so much when I needed it desperately, I'd do anything for him. I don't know what I would have done six years ago when my life blew up. I needed an escape and Jake provided it; by marrying me he gave me a new name, a new home, and a father for my unborn child. My emotional state was critical at that point of my life; I needed someone to lean on and Jake was there as he always had been for me in the past. Emma thinks Jake is her father and that is how it will stay. I'll always hold the worry she may find out the truth one day and resent me for not telling her about her real father, but he's such a terrible person and I don't want her to have someone like him in her life. Maybe my feelings will change when she's older and I'll tell her everything, but I doubt it.

I didn't realize how much Theo, Emma's father, had isolated me over our time together. I guess I made it easy for him. I already barely spoke to my parents due to other issues in my past, and as my relationship with Theo progressed, he became my main focus. He wanted all my attention and, in the beginning, I thought it was romantic and exciting, but it was only the early stages of control. Everything with him was such a whirlwind, a collection of intense highs and lows, but eventually the lows became much more frequent. Eight months into the relationship, I was fed up with his abusive control and all the secrets he kept from me. And then things got so crazy between us. I was almost three months pregnant and all I wanted was to get away from him. I had to protect my child.

Jake was the one friend I still spoke to, and I'd kept him secret from Theo knowing subconsciously that he'd flip out if he knew. But I'd talked to Jake at least once a week since I was ten and I would not give that up, even for Theo, who demanded all my attention. Jake is the one constant in my life and the person I trust the most. He's my best friend.

He rescued me. It sounds corny, but he was, and is, my hero. I left Pittsburgh, where my parents had moved to when I was sixteen, and moved in with Jake. He had broken up with his long-time girlfriend six months prior and said he was done with relationships. It was Jake's suggestion to get married, so I'd have a different last name if Theo ever tried to find me, and Jake who asked if he could be my baby's father.

It worked. We created a loving home for Emma and neither of us was interested in seeking out romantic relationships. For three years we worked, and we enjoyed spending time together and watching Emma grow. Then Jake met Candace at work. He fell in love with her and wanted to be with her. I'm so glad he found love again; he gave up so much for me and Emma. He deserves all the happiness in the world, and it seems like Candace is the one to give it to him.

Candace knows the basics, about me and Jake. It took a bit to convince her we never had a regular marriage, no physical or romantic involvement, only close friendship. We are a family, like a brother and sister. We all work together to make a seamless transition for Emma. Jake will always be her father, regardless of biological factors.

"Mommy, I'm hungry." Emma runs down the stairs. "Why's that man staring at our house?"

I stare at her. "What man?"

My daughter's big blue eyes widen. "I can see him from my bedroom window."

"Show me," I tell her, and we hurry up the stairs.

"Over there." She points to the school across the street.

I look in the direction she points, but I don't see anybody. I look to the right and the left, nothing. "I don't see anybody, honey."

Emma presses her lips together as she peers out the window. "I just saw him. He waved to me."

I survey the area again, but don't see anything, and a tremble of fear quickly runs through me.

Who did she see?

THREE

Him

I stand in the darkness, thick green shrubbery shrouding my presence, and enjoy the anonymity its protection provides as I monitor the property across the street.

It's a plain, unassuming house. Tan siding, cookie-cutter townhouse with a one-car garage, a small front porch, and a bright red front door. There are two windows on the first floor, and one larger window on the second floor—I know that's the daughter's bedroom. The curtains are closed tonight, but often they are open, affording me an easy view inside of mother and daughter in the kitchen on the lower floor and the cute daughter peeking out at me from the upper floor on occasion. A bright yellow planter sits to the left of the door, the dark red petunias spilling out of it illuminated by a dim porch light. A simple mailbox sits at the end of a short, paved driveway.

I know the woman who lives inside this nondescript house, some might say I know her well, but I'm not so sure anymore. I want to know her better, and what better way than watching?

It's amazing what people will reveal when they think no one is looking.

FOUR

Natalie

It's hard to believe we're mid-way through the second week of school, although it feels like summer still, with temps reaching the nineties today according to the weather report. I finally have our schedule finished. Abby and I have all of our students' needs covered throughout the school day, with a mix of inclusion in regular ed and small group instruction in our classroom. Schedules are bound to change, as they always do with new students, or a change in needs, but at least we have a solid starting point.

Plus, we have a new helper. The guidance counselor at the high school, Hannah Davenport, emailed me last week. They are doing a work study program for juniors and seniors interested in a career in education and offered our classroom a student helper for a few months, until the Christmas break. So this week Haley started. She comes in the afternoon, three days a week from twelve thirty to three thirty. She'll be helping me in Lucas's class, after which we bring three students to my classroom to complete independent work.

I'm navigating my way through Lucas's classroom, focusing on my students and keeping my interactions with him minimal and pleasant. Everything that happened between us, hurtful as it was, has been buried inside me for years. And that is where it will stay. I have enough to deal with in the present and certainly am not interested in digging out old skeletons from the past. I want to get through this school year and maybe next year another position may open that I won't have to work with fourth grade. The K-2 learning support teacher is expecting her second baby this spring and has been talking about quitting to stay home with her children.

I glance at the clock. About ten minutes until Haley and I take the students to my room. Mr. Hanson is writing the independent work assignment on the whiteboard, adjacent to the SMART Board.

"Mr. Hanson," I say, approaching him. "Do you have the worksheets for the second part that we will work on in my classroom?"

"Oh, yes, let me get those for you," he replies, walking to his desk at the back of the room.

"Mrs. Amaryllis!" Dylan calls, his hand up. I walk over to see what he needs. A minute later, girlish laughter erupts at the back of the room.

I look up. Lucas is standing by his desk with the worksheets in his hand. He's smiling at Haley, who has her hand on her hip and is laughing. He leans close to her, too close, and I watch as he whispers something in her ear.

"Mr. Hanson," she says playfully, "you're so funny."

His smile is playful too, even sexy, or am I imagining it? The interaction is over in a few seconds and then he's standing in front of me, placing the worksheets into my hand. He smiles at me too, but maybe less intensely than at Haley? Or am I simply imagining it?

"Cross out number twelve," he is saying to me. "I didn't get to cover that enough today, so we'll skip that one."

"Okay, great." I take the papers. "Heather, Dylan, and Sam, we're going to my room now. Make sure to bring your pencils and workbooks."

Haley joins us and we walk down the hall.

"You go ahead," I say to her. "I'll be there in a minute. I have to stop at the office to check my mailbox."

She nods, her long dark ponytail bobbing as she walks down the hall with our students. I wince internally as I recognize now how much Haley resembles me at that age. I enter the office and head toward the small room to the right of the secretary's desk that houses our mailbox cubbies and a copier. I don't need to check my mail. I just want to think about what I saw. If I even did see anything? I'm trying to keep an objective mind with Lucas, but something feels off here. The way he looks at Haley, the body language, all of it feels so predictable.

And I don't like it one bit.

I know what Lucas did with me is wrong. It was a violation of my innocence and his ethics as a teacher, a trusted adult, even though it didn't seem like that at the time. It took me years later to realize how he used me. He is ten years older than me, maybe not a big age gap when you're twenty-five and thirty-five, but fifteen and twenty-five is criminal. I sigh, still running the scene from the classroom through my mind, but I shouldn't allow my past experience to color the present. Surely nothing is happening with Haley. Lucas is forty-five years old and married. Haley is sixteen. I shouldn't project my past with Lucas into the present; it's a very different situation.

Although, he is still in a position of authority and the way he was talking to her, flirting with her, is not appropriate. But if I went to the principal, what would I say? They were laughing together? I keep thinking about what I witnessed, and uneasiness creeps into my stomach.

And I don't want to bring up my past with him. I need this job and I don't know how that would all play out. Lucas is incredibly charming, kind, gentle, and fun, but he could turn quickly when things weren't going his way or threatened what he wanted. He's like a spoiled peach, so lovely on the outside, but when you cut it open, rotten on the inside. If I told everything, maybe he'd lose his job, but it would take a long and difficult court case. And what would Emma and I do in the meantime? What if the exposure led Theo to us, and he somehow found out about Emma? All the outlandish possibilities run through my mind. My pulse races when I think of how things could turn out so badly for me and Emma. I force myself to calm down. It might have been nothing; I'll need to wait, see if I witness anything else.

I did check my mailbox in the office—a catalog of classroom educational manipulatives, and a chocolate bar from Daphne makes me smile. I make a mental note to repay her kindness next week with a treat in her mailbox.

I will stay alert and aware. If I need to report Lucas, I will, but I have to be careful how I do it. Depending on how things may go, I could be putting myself, and Emma, in danger. I don't care about myself; I know I'll survive.

But I can never put Emma in any chance of danger.

FIVE

Natalie

The dessert table is an array of brightly colored cupcakes, chocolate chip, oatmeal and sugar cookies, brownies, and a large three-layer cake sitting a bit lopsided on a cake stand. The treats sit atop a table covered with a red and white tablecloth, the school colors, and multicolored streamers around the table. Two bunches of helium-filled red and white balloons stand tall on each side of the table.

Hildy Bomberger is the PTA president and baker of the lopsided cake and probably the decorator of the table. I'm assigned to oversee the dessert table, and she made it clear that her cake should be the center of attention, although I don't know why; it doesn't have the best appearance. I grimace when she eyes me from the ball toss game across the cafeteria and walks in my direction. Great, now she wants to give me more directions.

"Mrs. Amaryllis," she says in a high-pitched tone. She smooths her strawberry blonde hair with her hand. I don't know why; it's already perfectly in place. "Please make sure my cake is displayed in the center of the table. I worked so hard on it."

I raise my eyebrows but don't say anything. Really? Is that why it's so lopsided and missing a clump of icing on the back? Did she even look at the cake she baked? I cannot *wait* to get dessert table duty over with and go home.

"Mrs. Bomberger, of course. Why don't you help me move it?" I ask. "It's a bit heavy."

Hildy laughs. "Oh, I would, but it's my turn to help with ball toss. Thanks!"

And then she is gone.

Damn Hildy. I push the cake stand, but it's too heavy, and it tips, the cake almost sliding off the stand. I pull it back and someone reaches their hands out, blocking the cake from falling further off the stand.

"Oops, I got it!" a soft female voice says.

I gently position the cake stand, and the woman pulls her hands back. Creamy buttercream frosting coats her pale lilac nails. I look up at her as she licks the icing from her fingers.

"Not bad, but Hildy needs to even out her baking pans," the young woman remarks.

I laugh. "You got that right." I hand her a napkin. "You might need this."

She laughs and wipes her fingers. "Thanks."

"I'm Natalie," I introduce myself. "Natalie Amaryllis."

"Nice to meet you, Natalie," she replies in a quiet tone. "I'm Olivia."

"Do you have a student here?" I ask, although she looks too young to have an elementary age student.

She shakes her head. "No, my husband is a teacher here. Lucas Hanson."

My smile freezes on my face. "Yes, I know Lucas."

She smiles at me, her eyes kind, her voice soft. "Everyone knows Lucas. He's around here somewhere."

I nod. Olivia, Lucas's wife, is very pretty and very young, just as Abby had said. Her hair is long, dark and wavy, like Emma's. Her porcelain skin, free of any blemishes, extends to an elegant long neck. Full red lips form a perfect bow and thick, perfectly arched eyebrows are above her crystal blue eyes. She wears a pale yellow sundress with a light white sweater and high-heeled sandals. She doesn't look much older than Haley.

"Well, thanks for saving the cake. Hildy would have killed me."

"Oh, for sure." Olivia laughs. "Dead on arrival."

I laugh. She's right.

"There you are." Lucas walks up behind Olivia, sliding his hand around her tiny waist. "Hi, Natalie, this is my wife, Olivia."

I nod. "Yes, we've met. She saved me from a cake disaster."

Lucas grins. "Hildy Bomberger?"

"Yes," says Olivia. We all laugh.

Lucas digs into his pocket and lays a five-dollar bill on the table. "Two chocolate chip cookies, please."

"You got it." I hand them the treats. I notice Lucas unwraps one and takes a bite but keeps the other one in his hand. Why doesn't he give it to his wife?

"We have to get over to the ice cream sundae bar," says Lucas. "We're on sprinkle duty."

I wave to them. "Nice meeting you, Olivia."

"You too, Natalie," Olivia replies, quietly, as they walk away.

The Back to School Carnival is in full swing. It was supposed to be held outside, but rain changed those plans. Now the cafeteria is full of game booths, face painting, various food offerings, and my dessert table, well really Hildy's dessert table.

Mrs. Farley, the math para, approaches the table. She raises her eyebrows. "I'm feeling daring; I'll take a piece of that lopsided cake."

I laugh. "Oh, you are daring!"

I cut a piece of cake and place it on a plate with a plastic fork. She takes a bite and smiles.

"Not bad," she says, laying some cash on the table. "Thanks, Mrs. Amaryllis."

"You're welcome," I reply as she walks away, nibbling on the cake.

Emma is still sitting at the face painting booth with her friend Becky, both girls having a butterfly painted on their face. I wave to her; she waves back and starts walking toward me, excitedly. Jake and Candace should soon be here too.

"Mommy." Emma runs over to me. "I'm a butterfly!"

"A purple butterfly!" I exclaim.

A line forms, everyone wanting cookies and cupcakes, although no more requests for Hildy's cake. She'll be so disappointed when she has to haul it home with her again.

"Did you bake all of these goodies?" a deep voice asks Emma.

She squeals and jumps up, running into Jake's arms. "Daddy!"

"Wow, I think you're happy to see me!" Jake remarks, picking her up and hugging her. "I missed you too."

"It's been three days!" Emma exclaims, holding up four fingers.

"I know, it's too long." He puts her down and slides his hand through his thick, sandy-colored hair. He directs his dark blue eyes to me. I've always been thankful he has blue eyes like Emma, and like her biological father, Theo. A little detail that fits our story of Emma being his child. "Hey, Nat."

"Hey, Jake." I smile. "About time you got here."

"I know, we were busy today."

"A rush on the accounting office? It's not even tax season."

"Don't remind me. But we're here now."

"Where's Candace?"

"I'm here," she says. Her dark red hair is pulled back in a barrette, slick from the rain outside. "Hi, Emma!"

"Hi, Candace."

A small frown flicks across Candace's face. It only lasts an instant, but I see it, although I'm not sure what warranted it. Uncertainty flickers inside me. I thought Candace and I were fine; there certainly isn't anything to be jealous of between us because of the nature of my relationship with Jake, but there's something I can't quite put my finger on about her that bothers me.

"Why don't you two take Emma to play some games and then come back to man the dessert table?" I suggest. "Then Emma and I will go to the dance party in the gym."

"Sounds fun," says Jake, taking Emma's hand.

"We'll be back in half an hour." Candace smiles at me.

"Great, have fun," I reply, watching them walk away, still wondering about that little frown I saw on Candace's face.

SIX

Olivia

I pour a heaping scoop of rainbow sprinkles on the sundae of a sweet blond-haired boy with a wide smile. His eyes widen and he scurries over to the cafeteria table to taste his treat. The ice cream sundae line is finally slowing down. When we first arrived the line snaked all the way to the back of the cafeteria.

"Natalie seems nice," I remark to Lucas, who keeps watching the clock on the wall.

"Yeah, she's nice. A bit skittish, but nice."

"Skittish?" I reply. "She didn't seem like that to me. Is this her first year here?"

"Yes."

"What school was she at before?"

Lucas shakes his head. "I don't know. We just talk about the students, nothing about our personal lives."

I raise my eyebrows. "That's unusual for you. You're usually in the mix of everything."

He looks at me now, his eyes narrowing slightly. "What's that supposed to mean?"

"You know what it means." I keep my tone light.

He stares at me for a moment, then laughs. "Maybe you're right. I don't know, Natalie is just quiet. Maybe she doesn't like me."

I move closer to him and lean up to whisper in his ear. "How could anyone not like you?"

He casts a knowing grin at me. "As long as you like me."

"You know I do."

He lingers close to me and whispers back. "Let's get out of here."

I pout. "What about the sprinkles?"

"I think the kids can manage," he says, his hand on the small of my back, leading me toward the door to the parking lot.

I stop in my tracks. "Hold on, I have to tell someone we're leaving."

"No, you don't, they'll figure it out," he says.

Mrs. Dell comes up to us and puts her hands on her hips. "Lucas Hanson, tell me you're not trying to sneak out of here."

Lucas laughs. "No, it's all Olivia's fault. Are you on sprinkle duty next?"

"Yes, I am." She surveys the half-empty sprinkle containers. "I may need some more."

"There's more in the kitchen," he says. "Have fun!"

He grabs my hand now and whispers to me. "Let's go before someone else starts talking to me."

I take one more glance at Natalie, still manning the dessert table. Something about her appeals. I'd like to say goodbye to her and maybe get her phone number to meet up some time; she seems like a nice person, and I don't have many friends here, but Lucas is ready to go.

So we go.

. . .

Lucas snores softly, his arms still around me, holding me close. I snuggle in, enjoying his body against me, his warmth, his protectiveness. I always feel safe with him. Nobody has ever made me feel safe like him. Even though our relationship has had its ups and downs, like most do, he's the only one I could ever count on. He's done so much for me.

I intertwine my hand with his and it reminds me of the first time he held me like this. I never felt so close to another person. He gave me the attention I craved for so long and being with him made me feel as if I had a future in life. If a man like him wanted me, I must be special and worthy of love. Our relationship started in a clandestine way, but when love finds you, that's it, no matter what the situation.

Lucas was my soccer coach in high school. I met him when I was sixteen, fell in love with him at seventeen and married him when I was eighteen. Now at twenty-four, I question some of the choices I made, but never my love for him. We've even been talking about possibly having a baby.

But sometimes, doubt creeps into my mind, particularly if I think about the facts without the feelings. I was a teenager, and he was a thirty-eight-year-old man. He was my coach. I cringe when I think about these cold hard facts, but then when the feelings roll in, all my logic changes.

Our relationship is special. Most people don't understand it, but that doesn't matter to me. It's about our feelings, not whether or not we fit into a perfectly wrapped box of logic, but rather a connection that is unexplained, yet incredibly real. He's the person I can confide in, the one who always makes me feel better, the one who I can always count on. He's my person.

Maybe it was taboo, at the time, but real love doesn't know age. That's what Lucas always tells me. And I believe him. He loves me and I know he wouldn't lie to me.

When we moved here six years ago, immediately after marrying, to care for his ill mother, I hadn't realized what a sizable task it would be to be a caregiver. For two years it consumed my life, leaving little time for anything else other than Lucas. It was such an isolating experience and even after his mother passed, I still struggled with making friends here. It doesn't help that Lucas doesn't want me to work, so my only social outlet to meet people is to volunteer at the school, but Lucas is happy and so am I.

At least that's what I tell myself.

SEVEN

Natalie

The next week at school I seem to be playing catch up with everything and today that meant copies that I should have made this morning but forgot. I hurry down the hall to the faculty room, a stack of papers in my hands, grasp the doorknob and step inside. All four tables inside the room are covered in baskets filled with various items and in the center table, a large roll of cellophane and a stack of bright red ribbons.

Olivia sits at the back table, wrapping a ribbon around a basket overflowing with numerous snacks.

"Oh, hi," she says in a shy voice. "Sorry for all the mess. I'm getting these ready for the raffle on Friday."

"No problem," I reply. "I just have some copies to make."

She smiles and looks down at the basket again. I go over to the copier, place my papers into the feed, select thirty copies of the packet of papers, stapled, and hit the button.

"Be careful of that copier," Olivia warns. "It's known for paper jams."

I laugh. "So I've heard."

A pause in the room, then Olivia asks in a quiet, pretty voice, "How do you like it here so far?"

"It's great, everyone is very friendly," I reply. "Do you often help out at school?"

She nods.

"I'm sure everyone appreciates your help," I say. "Especially your husband."

She smiles and walks over to another basket, wrapping cellophane around it. "I think he does."

I notice the hesitation in her voice and cast a glance at her. There's a softness about Olivia, a vulnerability, that's obvious. As beautiful as she is, she seems oblivious to it and perhaps lacking self-confidence. I shouldn't make assumptions though, I barely know her, though I'm sure that vulnerability in such a beautiful young woman is very attractive to Lucas.

My final packet emerges from the copier, and I grab my stack of papers.

"Have a good day," I say to Olivia as I turn to leave the room.

"Oh, um, wait a minute," she says in an unsure voice, fishing her phone from her purse. "Please, put your number in. Maybe we can go out for coffee or lunch sometime, if you want to?"

"Okay," I say, her request surprising me. I add my number. "That would be fun."

The week passes quickly and on Saturday afternoon, I pull into the driveway at Jake's house, a nice three-bedroom ranch home that used to be my own home for several years. The three of us shared many good times here, and now he's creating memories with Candace here. I approach the dark green front door and am about to ring the doorbell when I hear Emma shriek from inside.

"You're not my mom!" she's yelling.

I don't bother pressing the doorbell but turn the knob and am thankful when it opens. I'm standing in the doorway now, and Emma has tears running down her face and runs to me from the kitchen, into the living room.

"She doesn't have to call you mom if she doesn't want to. She has a mom." Jake's voice rises from the kitchen. "Don't push it."

"But I love Emma. Yes, Natalie's her mom, but she can call me mom too," Candace argues.

"Let it go!" Jake says.

"Mommy!" Emma cries. "I don't *want* to call Candace mom. You're Mom. She's Candace!"

Jake walks into the living room, shaking his head and leans down to Emma. "You don't have to, honey, if you don't want to."

"I won't!"

Candace appears in the doorway. A scowl covers her face when she stares at my daughter. Anger snakes through me. What is she thinking? Why would she even suggest this to Emma? She should have spoken to me first.

"Natalie, it's important to me that Emma knows how much I care about her. I think if she calls me mom, too, our bond will grow closer," she says earnestly.

"No!" I snap at her, more harshly than I intended.

"Hey," Jake intervenes. "Candace has good intentions. Even if it isn't the best idea, she feels strongly about it."

I glare at him. "She's not being fair to me. I don't know where all of this came from, but it stops now. Candace, you need to stop whining like a baby. The only opinion that matters here is Emma's."

"How dare you!" Candace yells. Her dark eyes blaze at me.

"Let's stop all this," Jake says. He turns to Emma. "Why don't you go outside to your swing set. I'll be outside in a few minutes."

"And then I go home with *Mommy!*" she says, looking at me.

"Yes," I reply. We all watch Emma open the sliding glass door and go out on her swing set.

"Natalie, this is important to me." Candace sighs.

"She's not calling you mom. I'm the only mom she has, and you should have brought this up with me before saying anything to Emma," I state.

"Let's just let it go. Maybe Emma will change her mind. It's up to her," Jake says, turning to me. "But you have to respect Candace's feelings too."

I glare at him. "What about my feelings?"

"Nat, you know this is a different situation. Just give Candace some slack. It can't always be about you."

Now I'm mad. Tears sting my eyes. "It's not about me. It's about Emma."

I push my tears back, gather myself, and go to retrieve Emma from the backyard. She says her goodbyes to them, and we walk out to the car. This is so stupid; I still don't know why Candace would even suggest it to Emma, and why doesn't Jake stick up for me more? I realize Candace is his wife, but she is wrong in this situation.

I grip the steering wheel the entire drive home. My head is pounding, and my body is swirling with emotions; I hate arguing and it seems as if hurdle after hurdle keeps showing up in my life.

I feel so alone.

The house is quiet. I peek in on Emma, sleeping soundly in her white canopied bed, snuggled beside her cherished stuffed bear and floppy green frog. Moonlight streams in from her bedroom window, and I quietly walk over to it, closing the curtains, giving a quick glance outside to the full moon glistening in the night sky.

I pad downstairs and put on a kettle for some hot tea. I flick on the TV, keeping it at a low volume, and put on a medical drama series I started watching last week. The argument with Candace and Jake still simmers in my mind. We'll have to sort things out between us, but I'm still angry.

A text pops up on my phone. I pick it up: Olivia, Lucas's wife.

> Hi Natalie, this is Olivia Hanson, are you busy?

I stare at it. Funny she's texting me at nine thirty on a Saturday night.

> Not really
>
> What are you doing?

The kettle gives a low whistle and I hurry to take it off the stove burner. I prepare my cup of tea and settle back on the sofa. A new text awaits.

> Nothing. Lucas played golf all day and he's asleep. Would you like to go out for a drink or something?

I laughed. My days of going out for a drink are long gone. Tea is about all I can handle these days.

> Sorry, my daughter is asleep.

> Oh, I didn't know you had a daughter. I'm sorry to bother you. You're probably spending time with your husband.

I laugh again. Definitely not.

> Nope, no husband. I'm divorced.

> So, you don't mind me texting you on a Saturday night. 😊

> Not at all. 🙂

A thought pops into my mind.

> Why don't you come over? I made tea.

Three dots.

> OK, what's your address?

I sent it to her.

> Don't ring the doorbell. Text me when you get here.

I sip my tea and now I feel a bit weird about inviting her over. Why did I ask Lucas's wife over to my house on a Saturday night? I barely know her; this is going to be a strange visit.

She arrives ten minutes later, so I guess she and Lucas don't live far away.

"Hi," I greet her at the door. "Come in. Do you want some tea?"

"Sure." Olivia smiles, shyly; her hair is up in a high ponytail. She wears comfy-looking sweatpants and a T-shirt.

"You don't look like you were ready to go out for a drink," I remark.

She laughs awkwardly. "I would have gotten ready pretty

quickly if you were game, but tea works too. I was kind of bored, so I thought I'd see what you were up to tonight."

"Your other friends were busy?" I ask. It was odd that she texted me. We only spoke at the carnival last Friday and a bit in the faculty room this week.

We sit down at the kitchen table to drink our tea. Olivia shakes her head. "I don't have many friends."

"That surprises me," I reply.

"Well, we moved here about six years ago right after we got married and it's just me and Lucas," she explains, her voice soft. "Sorry, maybe this is weird. I probably shouldn't have texted you. I'm friendly with some people at school because I volunteer there quite a bit, but no close friends here. This is really unusual for me. I'm not usually very outgoing. I don't know... I just wanted to get to know you better..."

I look at her, wringing her hands, obviously nervous and second guessing herself. "No, I'm glad you texted, it's a nice surprise. Yeah, it takes a while to make friends in a new place. Where do you work?"

"Um... I don't work; Lucas doesn't want me to," she says, taking a sip of tea.

I raise my eyebrows. "Really?"

"We moved here to take care of Lucas's mother. She had terminal cancer. I did a lot of the caregiving, and it was very stressful, especially since I was eighteen so I couldn't really work at the same time too." Her voice lowers.

"I can imagine that was stressful, and it makes sense that you'd need a break after something like that. You married Lucas where you were eighteen?" I remark. "So, you're twenty-four now?"

"I am." She looks at me. "I know what you're thinking."

I meet her gaze. I'm thinking that Lucas certainly never changed his penchant for teenage girls. Although I had thought she was probably closer to thirty, but just looked younger.

"What?"

"Our age difference is substantial," she remarks. "But love has no age."

Love has no age. I remember Lucas telling me the same when we met secretly in his coaching office located conveniently at the end of a long, lonely hall past the girls' and boys' locker rooms. The only other space in the hall was a huge utility closet, making his office very private, especially when the shades were drawn, and the door was locked.

Apparently, he used the same lines with her. How original.

I pull myself together. "No, I was wondering how long you cared for Lucas's mother."

"She died about two years later. We had moved in with her when we got here." She sighs. "It was a stressful couple of years for a lot of reasons."

I nod. "I can imagine. What did you do after she passed?"

"After being Marion's caregiver for a little over two years, Lucas wanted me to relax, take time to redecorate the house—we inherited it—and just enjoy myself," she says, in her quiet way. "Lucas is so, um, particular that I look a certain way. The stress was very unhealthy for me. I was eating so much junk food and wasn't taking care of myself."

I look at her. "Well, caring for a terminally ill woman is an intense job for anyone, especially a young woman with no experience in that field. Why didn't Lucas hire a nurse to help you?"

"He did, but she only came a couple days a week." She's pensive for a few moments. "It was a really hard job; I don't know why he didn't do more himself. She was his mother. I think he found it too tough."

I nod, but I'm not sure Olivia notices. It's almost as if she's speaking to herself, not me. This conversation has gotten very personal, very fast, but it seems as if she just needed someone to talk to.

"In my opinion, that's a great deal of responsibility to take on and it's pretty impressive that you handled it so well," I say, smiling at her. "It's a lot to share for a first conversation. We barely know each other, but I feel I learned a lot about you in a short time."

Olivia nods. "Yeah, sorry if I seem kind of off, I just haven't thought about that time of my life for a long time. I don't normally talk this much to people I don't know well. Please don't think I'm strange, but I felt like we could be friends. Real friends. Am I being strange?" She laughs nervously. "I probably am."

"A little," I admit gently. "But I know what you mean. I feel comfortable with you. I'm sure we'll be great friends."

I stare at her, still twitching her hands, although not as vigorously as earlier. I mean, it is strange to me to be sitting here talking about such personal things with the wife of the man who groomed me, but she appears to need someone to talk to and I'm happy to do so. She seems like a very sweet person.

"Good, but that's enough about me," Olivia says. "So, you have a daughter?"

"Yes, Emma's five. I'm recently divorced and we're adjusting to that change."

"Big change."

"Yeah, had a bit of an argument earlier today with my ex's new wife. She wanted Emma to call her mom, but Emma refused."

"No way, that's not right!"

"No, it's not. And it made me so angry. I don't know why Candace is pushing it so much."

"I'm sorry you had to deal with that. Maybe she just wanted to be included in the family and thought that was a way to do it."

"Maybe."

"I can see why that would bother you though, and if your

daughter doesn't want to call her mom, hopefully she'll let it go. What does your ex say?"

"He agrees. It's Emma's choice."

"That's good," says Olivia. "Maybe just talk to Candace and work it out. You don't want to be constantly arguing or irritated with her."

"No, I don't." I drink the rest of my tea. "You give pretty good advice."

"My specialty." Olivia's blue eyes sparkle, her body relaxing now. "I'm so glad you invited me over tonight."

I smile at her. "So am I."

EIGHT

Olivia

The streets are empty as I drive home from Natalie's house. Not surprising; it is after midnight. I'm still smiling, thinking about our visit. I'm glad I texted Natalie tonight. I can't explain it, but I feel a connection to her; I'm drawn to her for some reason. I hope I may have found my first real friend here; it's been so long since I've had a girlfriend, not since high school. For the last six years, everything has been about Lucas.

The conversation I had with Natalie about caring for Marion, Lucas's mother, still lingers with me. I realize a little guiltily that I hadn't thought about her in a while, but I reflect now that I was very young to be her carer. I never stopped to wonder why Lucas wanted to get married so quickly. Of course I didn't want to question it. I was desperate to marry him, to change my life. And boy did it change. We got married and the next month we moved in with Marion, and that was my life for the next couple of years.

Why haven't I ever thought about this before?

I haven't had a friend since I've been serious with Lucas.

Maybe that's why. He's the only one I talk to about serious things. Maybe he frames topics so that I see them as he wants me to.

In the safety of the car, driving down quiet, dark streets, I let myself think the big scary thought that's been plaguing me recently. My life with Lucas has become increasingly small. Too small. I need a friend. Maybe I should get a job? I've thought about it, of course, but I don't know what I'd do. I don't want to be a caregiver or work at a donut shop, which is my only other job experience. And I know exactly what Lucas will say. Will I have time to work out at least an hour every day, do my skin treatments, what about volunteering at the school, what about preparing healthy meals? He is preoccupied with keeping me looking youthful and healthy, so much so I feel like his doll sometimes, rather than his wife. Something he can take out and play with, and then put me back on the shelf when he's done. Working has never seemed worth the hassle before, as Lucas has a good job, and we had inherited some money, and the house, from his mother, so I don't *need* to work.

But I need something for myself.

I admire Natalie. She's smart, fun and I love how she talks about her daughter and her job; obviously she loves both very much. I imagine it must be a wonderful feeling to have a career that you love and feel excited about. I feel inspired by her; she's so confident and sure of herself, two weak areas for me. I hope I can be a mother like her one day. The career thing probably won't happen for me, but I know I can be a good mother.

The joy from that idea wins over my disloyal thoughts. I shouldn't complain about Lucas. He's my world, and hopefully, soon to be the father to my baby. Where would I be without him? I'm not strong and smart like Natalie. Like my mother used to say, "It's a good thing you're pretty because you don't have the brains." Although she wasn't a rocket scientist, so I don't know what she was basing her assessment on exactly.

My thoughts fill with memories of Lucas. I loved him from the first moment I saw him. And I loved how he saw me. He listened so intently to me, really listened to what I had to say. When he talked to me, he gave his full attention and it was so empowering, I felt like I mattered for the first time.

I thought I was the luckiest girl in the world when Lucas turned his attention to me when he started coaching my soccer team. He was so good-looking; all the girls had a crush on Coach Hanson. He was a good coach, patient, and kind. And he was so funny, he always made me laugh. It was unbelievable that he wasn't married or in a serious relationship. He was easy to talk to and I shared things with him about my family and life that I shared with no one else. Talking to him made me feel safe and important.

One day after practice, I stayed later after the rest of the girls left, helping him put the soccer balls and other gear into the utility closet by his office. When we were finished putting the equipment away, he touched my hand before I opened the closet door to leave. I stared at his hand, gently rubbing mine, and then our fingers intertwined. I looked at him, and he asked if he could kiss me. Excitement rushed through me, and I nodded, almost feeling paralyzed in that moment. I'd been thinking about kissing him for months but never thought it would ever happen. It was soft, gentle at first, then increased in intensity. His hands ran slowly down my body. Only kissing that day, but by the following week, we were in his office with the door locked and the blinds closed. He had a comfortable couch in there and while I was nervous at first, those nerves quickly dissipated.

I had some experience with boys, but that experience didn't compare to being with Lucas. I'd be dizzy with anticipation and desire by the end of soccer practice, eager for the other girls to go home. The intense looks throughout practice only intensifying what I knew would come after everyone left. Some of the other girls noticed a closeness, something different between us, and I pulled away from my friends, somewhat; I only wanted to spend my time with Lucas, alone, further exploring this incredible attraction between us.

He's different now than he used to be, or maybe it's just that I know him now, and he was probably always this way. My thoughts travel to last week when I was making dinner.

"Olivia, what's this?" Lucas had demanded, staring into the trash can in the kitchen. He reached inside and pulled out a discarded plastic bag.

I stared at him for a moment. "Uh, the bag the carrots were in. I cut some up for your lunch today."

He knew what a carrot bag was, so why was he acting so strange?

He frowned. "I thought something tasted off with those carrots. These are not organic. I told you to only buy organic."

I stared at the bag and he was right, I'd made a mistake. Normally I did buy organic carrots but I'd been rushing yesterday when grocery shopping.

"Oh... sorry," I said.

Lucas huffed and threw the bag back into the trash. "Get it right next time. I don't want to eat *regular* vegetables."

Now, I think about how particular, even controlling, Lucas is even over something as small as carrots. I love him but I don't like this side of him.

Yes, he's my world. I hope I'm his too, but there's nothing wrong with me having something for myself too, is there? I've only begun to realize this lately, these strong stirrings for something of my own, separate from Lucas, something only for me, but I'm not sharing this with him yet. I'm certain he will have strong feelings about the topic.

. . .

The nail tech massages my legs and applies more lotion to them. We were chatting about movies earlier, but Nina knows I like to close my eyes and relax while she massages and then applies the nail polish.

I love coming to the salon. Who doesn't love pedicures, massages, and beauty treatments? And I like talking to everyone who works here too; they're really the only people I see on a regular basis, other than Lucas. What I don't like is how Lucas schedules my appointments and reminds me about them. Today, before he went to work, he suggested I pick a shade of blue for my nails this afternoon. He always seems to track and remember my appointments before I've even thought about them. I felt like a queen when he started booking them for me after we first got together, but now it annoys me. I tell him I can make my own appointments, but he insists on doing it and it seems pointless to argue.

Maybe I'm being too particular. I'm sure most husbands don't schedule their wife's salon appointments, so maybe I should just be happy and enjoy the treatments no matter who does the scheduling.

I sometimes get sick of my thoughts. Am I just a spoiled housewife with nothing else to complain about? Well, I know that's not true. Nina continues to rub my calves and it feels heavenly. The lavender-scented moisturizer is a pleasure too.

"Okay, did you choose a nail color?" Nina asks.

I open my eyes and look at her. "Yes, I'm going with Razzle Red today. Going to try something different."

I smile watching her paint the bright red polish on my toenails.

Change, even in small doses, is progress.

Even nail polish.

NINE

Natalie

I peek in the oven at my French toast casserole, brown sugar bubbling on top. I open the fridge and retrieve a bowl of cut-up strawberries and the carton of orange juice. The bacon sits draining on a paper towel, crisp and brown. My stomach rumbles.

"Daddy's here!" Emma comes tearing down the stairs. "I saw him from my window."

"Good, the food's ready," I say as the doorbell rings. I wipe my hands and go to answer it.

Jake is joining me and Emma for brunch. Candace is away today, shopping with her mother and sister. I'm glad we'll have some time together to talk alone, especially after that fiasco over at their house the other day. It will be easier to talk to Jake without Candace around.

I open the door, and Jake hands me a bouquet of bright sunflowers. I accept them and smile at him.

"Are we good?" he asks. "Sorry about what I said. I don't want to argue."

"Neither do I," I reply. "Yes, we're good."

We walk into the kitchen, and Emma claps when she sees the sunflowers. "Pretty!"

"Yes, they are." I pull a vase from the kitchen cabinet, fill it with water, and add in the flowers.

"I was just trying to keep the peace," Jake says, sitting down at the table. He pops a strawberry in his mouth.

"I'm going to get my Barbies to sit with me." Emma runs back upstairs.

"I know you're in a tough spot," I say, making sure Emma is out of earshot. "But if Emma doesn't want to call her mom, she doesn't have to. And I don't want her to either."

"I know." He nods. "Candace understands that now. I think she's looking for a way to be closer to Emma."

"Emma adores Candace. She really does." I pause. "I'll call her and talk to her. Hopefully that will smooth things out. I don't want any tension between us."

"Neither do I," Jake replies. "Wow, I'm glad you said that. I thought you'd be mad."

"I was at first, but not anymore," I say. "You know how happy I am for you. I'll do whatever I can to make Candace feel like a member of the family. I'll do it for you because I want you to be happy and I think we all just want a peaceful life."

"Thank you, I really appreciate it." He walks over to snag a piece of bacon. "I never thought I'd want another relationship, but then I met Candace."

"You never know when you'll find love."

"What about you?" he asks. "Are you ready to start dating again?"

I shake my head. "No, I'm focusing on Emma and my job, that's it. I think I'd like a partner in the future, when Emma is older, but not now. And you know my track record. I don't make the best choices in men."

"Geez, that's true. So, nobody interesting at your new job?"

"No, um... I didn't tell you but guess who works at the school?"

"Who?"

"Lucas Hanson. He teaches fourth grade."

Jake chokes on the bacon. He grabs a glass of juice and gulps it down. He looks at me. "The guy that raped you?"

I frown. I hate when he uses that word. When I think of rape, I think of a violent physical assault, and it wasn't like that with Lucas. Manipulation, mind games, emotional violation, yes, but I know why he uses that term.

"You know I hate when you say that."

"I know, but he did. You were fifteen and he was an adult and your *coach*. It was statutory rape."

"I realize that now. It's so strange seeing him, but he doesn't recognize me. He just thinks I'm a new teacher."

"He doesn't even recognize you?" Jake groans. "Oh, this guy is trash."

"I'm glad he doesn't recognize me. I just want to do my job and live a quiet life."

"You have a complicated life." He lets out a sigh.

"I do." I pour a cup of coffee and hand it to him, then refill my mug. "At least I have one friend who knows all about it."

"And he's your ex-husband." He laughs.

"I really do have a complicated life," I reply, laughing with him.

I turn off the lamp next to Emma's bed and snuggle next to her. I stroke her hair, and she lets out a yawn, stretching her little arms high into the air. Moonlight streams through an opening in her curtains, giving light to her Barbies strewn across the floor and her dollhouse that sits behind them.

"I love you," I whisper to her. "Sweet dreams."

"Stay till I fall asleep," she mumbles.

"Okay."

"Mommy?"

"What?"

"Who is the man outside?"

I look at her. "What man?"

"The man in the baseball cap; he looks at the house," she says as sleep colors her voice.

A fizzle of panic shoots through me. Who is she talking about? I never noticed a man watching our house. This is the second time she has said a man is watching our house. He would have to be standing at the school entrance if he was across the street, or did she mean in our front yard?

"Honey, when did you see this man?"

"Last night." She's barely awake now. "And... tonight."

Tonight.

Her breathing slows and she rolls over with her bear, now asleep. I get out of bed and go over to her curtain. Emma's bedroom is at the front of the house, facing the road and the school. You can see the driveway and our small front yard. The outdoor lights at the school light up the area, but there are pockets of dark areas where a person may lurk. I must stand at the window for fifteen minutes, but I don't see anything unusual.

I let the curtain fall closed and turn to look at my daughter again. Probably nothing. Maybe a man was working on something at the school and was looking across the street at our house. The school often has landscapers working on the flower beds around the front, and there was an issue with the roof last week so there were some men working up there. I'm sure there is a simple explanation.

A chill runs up my spine as I walk downstairs and start tidying up the kitchen. Thoughts of Theo fill my mind and thoughts of Lucas. Neither one of them would have a favorable view of me, but Theo would certainly be the most dangerous. I want to push those unsettling thoughts away but struggle to do so. I quickly close the open curtains on the window above the kitchen sink.

Is someone watching me?

Watching us?

TEN

Him

The light in the upstairs bedroom shines bright. Natalie must be reading her daughter a bedtime story; what a good mother. I watch the bedroom, remembering earlier, when the little girl had watched me from the same window. It wasn't the first time she'd seen me; she's quite observant for a young child. More so than her mother, who is obviously concerned with other issues.

The light suddenly goes out and I slink into the shrubbery, becoming one with them to hide my presence. The window is dark, but I feel her looking, perhaps for me? Did her daughter mention she saw me? A smile crosses my face, delight in her thinking about me fills my mind, and I sigh. I rather enjoy the thought of her searching for me now, wondering who could be watching her and her young daughter. She will wonder who it is out here, lurking in the tall shrubbery, gathering information about her and her daughter. What they like to do. Their daily routine. Oh, I find all of it so interesting.

What will I do next?

Will I allow her to see me?

Oh no, not yet. It's not time. I'll know the right time when it arrives, but for now I'm happy to slink around under the cover of night, hidden by black clothing and hooded sweatshirts. All the sneaking around is fun to me. It's been some time since I've watched anyone in this manner.

The night air holds a crispness that's common in an early autumn evening. I inhale deeply allowing the oxygen to fill my lungs and then exhale. I've spent many nights out here observing this home, its lights and windows, its comings and goings, its inhabitants. Some may call it a waste of time, but I view it as an investment of time, knowledge but mostly...

An investment in her.

ELEVEN

Natalie

I crawl into bed, rubbing moisturizer into my hands. I glance at the clock and decide to call Candace and mend fences. I wait a few minutes, allowing the lotion to dry on my hands; I'm not exactly in a hurry to talk to her. In fact, I dread doing it, but it needs to happen so I might as well get it over with and enjoy the rest of my evening. It's only a few minutes after nine. I grab my cell phone. She answers on the first ring.

"Hi, Natalie."

"Hey, Candace," I say in a friendly voice. "Just wanted to touch base with you. I don't want to argue and hope things are good between us now."

She coughs. "Sure, I agree. I crossed the line with Emma. I shouldn't have asked her to call me mom. I'm sorry."

"Emma loves you, Candace, so much! And she loves spending time with you," I reply.

There's a pause. "I'm so glad, and thank you for calling me. It means a lot."

"Of course, have a good evening."

"Same to you. Good night." Candace hangs up the phone.

Hmmm... I lay my phone down on the nightstand. Candace said the right words, but I don't think she meant them. Hopefully all of this will just blow off and things can get back to normal.

Well, I tried, and I'll leave it at that.

I'm not going to allow Candace to take up any more time in my thoughts.

I rise from the bed and open my closet door. I bend down, rummage in the back under a couple of shoe boxes for an old backpack, unzip it and pull out a plastic Target bag and then the small leather bag inside. I open it and touch the neat packs of cash. I sniff them; I rather like the scent of cash, even if it is dirty. And this cash, it's the dirtiest of all.

The smooth bills are cool to my touch. The bag used to be stuffed to the brim. Fifty thousand dollars originally, but now it's closer to thirty thousand, after I needed to use some to purchase a car, and other expenses that came up over the past five years. This little bag of cash proved to be a lifesaver. My insurance policy when I fled Pittsburgh, and Theo. He doesn't need it; he is in jail, for now. I took a chance sneaking it into my suitcase the day before I left and taking it with me to school. He was out on bail, then, posted by Bobby, his business partner. I was told they were investment bankers, but then found out armed robbery was their business. Theo was scrambling to hide his money before his court date, although he was certain he wasn't going to jail.

Robbery isn't the reason Theo is in jail.

I flick through the bills. I was desperate when I left, no job, pregnant and scared. My only flicker of hope was Jake. I took that money for me and for my baby. Theo's baby. The cash has been needed over the last few years. I have never regretted taking it, even if it was ill gotten.

Theo owes me that much.

. . .

We file into the gymnasium with all grades four through six. We're having a reptile assembly and I hope our class is seated toward the back. Some of the other teachers mentioned the presenter was known to "volunteer" people to hold various creatures.

"Okay, class, sit here behind Mrs. Dell's class," Lucas directs. The students fill in and sit on the floor, crisscross applesauce.

I sit on a chair at the side and Lucas sits beside me, closest to his class. Haley sits on the floor, next to a student.

"Haley, there's a chair here," I say, pointing to an empty folding chair.

"Miss Haley is sitting next to me!" Heather exclaims, a wide smile on her freckled face.

"Yes, I am." Haley beams at her. She waves me off. "I'm fine. I'll sit with the class."

I shrug my shoulders. "Okay."

Lucas glances at her sitting next to him on the floor beside Heather, and a sly smile crosses his face.

"Welcome, everyone!" the presenter announces at the front of the gymnasium. "My name is Devon and I have some amazing creatures to show you today!"

The classes cheer and clap as he goes behind a dark green curtain and emerges with a long yellow and white snake around his neck. Oh, great, please don't come my way.

"This handsome young man is Stewart," Devon says. "He's two years old and a good friend of mine. He's an albino Burmese python and very friendly."

Devon walks across the front of the gymnasium full of students as they ooh and ahh at Stewart. "I think Stewart would like to get to know some of you a little bit better. Maybe one of the teachers would like to hold him?"

Here we go.

The students roar with excitement. He walks over to our side. Oh, great. Luckily, he stops at Miss Hanigan, a fifth-grade teacher, who shakes her head. I don't blame her.

Then Lucas jumps up from his chair. He runs a hand through this thick, dark hair and raises his hand. "Devon, I'd love to hold Stewart."

"Oh, perfect!" Devon exclaims. "And your name?"

"Mr. Hanson," Lucas replies.

All the students and staff clap. "Okay, Mr. Hanson, come up here and greet Stewart properly."

Lucas raises his hands in the air and walks toward Devon and Stewart, obviously enjoying the attention of the crowd as everyone claps. Haley gets up from the floor and sits in the seat next to me that Lucas had occupied, I guess to get a better view. She stares at him like everyone else in the room.

An old memory pops into my mind. I was a sophomore in high school and there was a pep rally for the football team in the gym. Everyone was there, cheering and clapping because the game that night determined the state championship.

Lucas was there that day. He filled in for the football coach when he had emergency surgery, pulling double duty as football and soccer coach for a short time. He'd called me the night before to let me know he'd be there and not to take the bus; he'd take me home later.

I sat in the bleachers with my friends and teammates from the soccer team and watched him join the football team on the floor and speak at the podium. His speech was electrifying, and he held everyone's rapt attention. All eyes on him. We'd been dating, if you could call it that, for a couple months and I was mesmerized by him, not only how he kept the crowd's attention, but by absolutely everything about him.

My feelings for him overwhelmed me. I thought about him constantly and hung on to everything he said to me, every touch he gave me and every sweet whisper of his still lingered in my ears. I saw him like everyone in that pep rally saw him and everyone in this assembly. Outgoing, friendly, dashing, a real showman, someone you can't take your eyes off for a moment because you don't want to miss anything. Most of all I loved how he listened to me, gave me his full attention whenever we talked. It's a skill not everyone possesses to make someone feel as if every word they speak is important and to give input to the thoughts they utter. He made me feel seen and that's powerful at any age, but especially at fifteen years old. Nobody in the gym that day knew about those qualities of Lucas; they only saw the magnetic, handsome man in front of them.

And he was mine.

I thought he was at the time. A few months later, that thought changed dramatically.

Lucas accepts the snake from Devon and appears happy and comfortable as Stewart slinks around his neck. He smiles, gleaming white teeth, against a still devastatingly handsome face.

"Peyton Heights East Elementary School!" His voice soars. "It's Stewart and Mr. Hanson!"

"Mr. Hanson!" The students cheer. Everyone is laughing and cheering, except Haley, who sits still in the chair next to me.

"He's really something, isn't he?" she says to me in a low voice.

"Yeah, he's something," I reply.

Her look disturbs me.

The same look I had so many years ago.

TWELVE

Natalie

Friday afternoon we do math centers in Mr. Hanson's classroom. I'm at the front table doing a fraction game, and Lucas is at the back table doing a word problem game. There's also a math card game students are playing as partners, and an iPad independent workstation. Students have twenty-minute rotations at each station. Haley monitors students doing partner games and independent work.

"Your turn, Heather," I say, handing her the dice.

Heather rolls the dice and moves her game piece seven spots. She studies the fraction problem and hesitantly gives the answer.

"That's correct, great job, Heather!" I praise her. "Okay, Phillip, you're next."

I glance up to check on Haley. She's standing by Mandy's desk explaining something to her on the iPad. She is doing such a good job with the students. I'm so proud of her; she's going to make a great teacher. She's been a wonderful addition to our team, and I'll miss her when she leaves in December. At the same time though, I can't wait for that to happen, for her to be out of Lucas's sphere.

"Okay, Todd, take your time. Think about what we learned yesterday." Lucas's voice carries up to me from the back of the room.

I look at him sitting at the back table with his small group of students. The students' attention is on the game they are playing, but Lucas isn't looking at them or the game spread out in front of them.

He's staring at Haley, who's now bent over Mandy's desk doing something on the iPad. He must feel my stare because a few moments later, he directs his gaze to me. Surprise flits across his face for a moment, then he smiles as the timer goes off, indicating a change of center rotations.

The student groups move to their next center. Lucas is busying himself with the next group, avoiding my gaze, since I caught him checking out Haley. His boldness doesn't surprise me, but it does disturb me.

I've been keeping Haley always in my sight, and I'm going to have to keep being vigilant of her whereabouts while she is here. I'm going to have to talk to her too, make sure she can come to me if something, or someone, is making her uncomfortable.

I don't trust Lucas.

Not for one minute.

Abby left early today for a doctor's appointment, so it's a perfect time to speak to Haley. I wait patiently as she talks to Anna at the back of the classroom, looking through a few sheets of stickers. Haley helps Anna put a sticker on her chart and waves to her as she leaves the classroom. She turns to me; excitement covers her face.

"Anna is so sweet, isn't she? I just love coming here."

I return her smile. "And we love having you here, Haley. You're so good with the students."

She beams, pushing back a lock of dark hair. "Thank you, Mrs. Amaryllis!"

"Oh, you can call me Natalie. At least when students aren't around."

She giggles and touches her face. "That's what Mr. Hanson said too. Lucas."

I stare at her. "When did he say that?"

"Um... today. Actually, just like half an hour ago in the faculty room when I went down for a bottle of water."

"What else did he say?"

She flashes me a look. Am I being too odd?

"He was getting a water too. His class was at their special. I think he said it was art class today."

"Anything else?"

She shakes her head, but her face says otherwise. She's keeping something from me.

"Nothing else?"

"No." Her face changes and now she's looking at me oddly. "That's it."

"Okay, well now that I think about it, I think you should continue to call me Mrs. Amaryllis and continue to call him Mr. Hanson. It's more professional."

"Okay." Haley now wears a confused expression on her face. "Are you okay?"

"Yes," I reply, but I'm flustered. "Haley, please tell me if you ever feel uncomfortable here, or if anyone is making you feel uncomfortable."

"Okay." She nods.

"Does Mr. Hanson make you feel uncomfortable? I don't mean just today, anytime. If he does let me know."

She shakes her head. "No, not at all."

I stop because I can tell the only one making her feel

uncomfortable is me. I want her to trust me. She's already looking at me like I've lost it, so if I keep blathering on, she's only going to tune out what I'm saying.

"Great. I'm so proud of the work you are doing here. We are so lucky to have you here."

"Thanks, Mrs. Amaryllis." Haley smiles, glancing at the clock. "Okay, well I have to go. Have a good weekend!"

"You too! See you next week!" I call as she walks out the door.

Well, that went *real* well.

Today is the Annual Fun Run at school and the temperature is hot which is good for the water games, but that's about it. It's one of those sticky, humid September days when the air is so thick you feel as if you could cut through it with a knife. The students run around the soccer field for half an hour, but you don't have to run; walking is okay too, or skipping as some students prefer to do. The grades will take turns with the run/walk, an obstacle course, and a few water games on the basketball court round out the activities.

Quite a few parent volunteers are here today helping with the games and manning the snack table sponsored by the PTA. I hope Hildy didn't bake any more lopsided cakes. But at least I wouldn't have to help her keep it on the plate if she did; I have other assigned duties today. The high school also sent some volunteers to help, including Haley.

Abby and I monitor the obstacle course. Haley and a few other high school students join us, including a blond-haired boy who seems much more interested in Haley than anything else.

The grass is freshly cut and despite the air being warm, it's also humid and the grass is a bit wet; pieces of it clump to our sneakers. The sky is blue without even a hint of a cloud visible. I'm not much of an outdoor person, so I'll be glad when these activities are over, and we can go back into the cool, air-conditioned school.

"Where are we putting these orange cones?" Haley asks, holding a stack of them.

"Oh, put them over there, right after the hula hoops and before the tunnel," I direct.

"I'll help you, Haley," the blond guy says.

"Okay, thanks, Rick." She smiles at him.

Hmmm... maybe Haley has a boyfriend I haven't heard about; that would be wonderful news. I watch the two set up the cones, laughing and whispering to each other. Maybe I don't have to worry about Lucas after all; maybe Haley and Rick are an item. I'm going to ask her about him later.

I think about the conversation I had with Haley about Lucas and I hold no doubt that she is comfortable with him, too comfortable; that's the problem. Lucas is one of the most engaging people I've ever met and once he sets his sights on you, he's hard to resist, almost impossible. You truly believe everything that he tells you. Probably because the only ones he sets his sights on are vulnerable young girls. Before you know it, you're ensnared in his web, unable to get out, until he cuts you loose.

Or am I overthinking the whole situation?

I wave to Olivia, who's manning the PTA snack table with Hildy, who is meticulously arranging the bags of potato chips and pretzels along with rearranging the water bottles and juice boxes in the coolers. A large white box sits on the table, allegedly filled with some of Hildy Bomberger's famous cupcakes. Apparently, cupcakes are her specialty, not cakes.

My friendship with Olivia is developing at a record speed. I like her and I feel she really needs a friend. As much as she says how much she loves Lucas, I hear those cracks in her voice and I'm probably the only one who understands what she's not telling me. She's trapped with him, but I don't think she's aware of it yet.

"Here's some more cones they want us to set up," Abby says, both arms full.

"Give them to Haley and her friend Rick." I point over to them where they're still talking; only a few cones are set up, they're so preoccupied.

"I didn't know she had a boyfriend," Abby remarks. "He's a cute boy. They make a cute couple."

"I don't know if he's her boyfriend, but they seem friendly," I reply.

Abby laughs. "Hey, go get yourself one of the cupcakes at the snack table, chocolate with peanut butter frosting. There's nothing like a Hildy Bomberger cupcake!"

"Really," I say. "Well, I guess I have to try a famous Bomberger cupcake."

"Get me one, too, please!" she says. "Or just wait until I give these to Haley, then I'll walk over with you."

She approaches the two, giving them the additional orange cones. Rick takes them, and the two set them up on the obstacle course. Haley pulls her phone from the back pocket of her shorts, stares at it, then begins typing. She says something to Rick, then walks away from him to a grove of trees by the side of the soccer field.

Abby and I walk over to the snack table to get a bottle of water and a Bomberger cupcake, then I notice Olivia is staring at something behind me; at first, I thought she stared at me, but I wave, and she doesn't notice.

I turn around to the direction of her gaze and see Lucas, no longer walking with his class, but standing off to the side by the soccer goal furiously texting on his phone. He looks agitated.

Olivia's gaze moves from him to Haley, standing under the grove of trees, still texting. She's facing the trees, so her back is to us and I'm unable to see her expression as she types.

Are they texting each other?

THIRTEEN

Olivia

I page through the stack of college brochures sitting on our dining room table. I've been looking through them most of the afternoon and, I must admit, feel a bit excited about the possibility of starting something new. A million ideas and questions race through my mind.

The door from the garage opens and slams shut. I hear Lucas walk inside and open the refrigerator.

"Hey, Olivia," he calls. "What's for dinner?"

I sigh. He asks the same thing every day he gets home from school. Normally I'm the happy homemaker and I have some delicious dinner ready for him. It makes him so happy. But I got caught up in my reading. I don't care about dinner. "I'm in the dining room."

He walks in and stares at me. "Why are you in here?" He glances at the stacks of brochures. "What's all this?"

"College brochures," I reply.

He cocks his head. "Oh, why?"

I sigh. "I think I'm going to enroll somewhere. I could do online, but I think I'd enjoy going to a physical classroom."

Lucas shakes his head. "What are you talking about? Why would you do that?"

I stare at him. "I want something for myself. I need something. My life can't all be about you."

"It's not. It's about you too. You have things you do for yourself." He laughs. "Come on, most women would love to have a schedule like yours. I mean, you go to the gym, the salon and you make dinner, that's a really nice day. I'd like that kind of day. What do you have to complain about, Olivia?"

Of course he doesn't understand. Yes, my life is comfortable, but I need something else. I need something that is just mine. I have to do something, but I don't know exactly what, yet. Why doesn't he understand that I need something more in my life than just him? Something that makes me feel like my own person, not just his wife. But I don't want to start conflict between us; I hate arguing with Lucas.

He always wins.

"And college, that's not something you were ever interested in anyway," he says, pushing the brochures away from me.

I look back at the stack of brochures, feeling a little sad about them now even though I was so excited only moments earlier. Wasn't I? There was a time when I thought about it, dreamed of going, but I didn't know how I'd do it. I certainly didn't have the parental support. When I got involved with Lucas, everything happened so fast and we were married before I knew it, right after graduation, and then moving in with his dying mother; we didn't even have a honeymoon. Then it was my job to care for her while he was working or away, which was *a lot*. She was a nice woman, but I was eighteen and didn't want to be a sick woman's caregiver. Regardless, I did it for Lucas, and in the beginning, it was only supposed to be while he was working. We had a visiting nurse come in too, but that was only a couple days a week. Suddenly Lucas had such a busy schedule, tutoring, meetings, etc., so many responsibilities he always said. All I know is that I was practically chained here caring for his mother and he was always gone. That experience was so isolating, and I resented how he left me here by myself for hours to care for his mother. But I had married him, and he made it seem as if this was somehow my duty. I proved how much I loved him and I'd do it again... I think.

"I did want to go to college. Remember how good I was at math in school?" I reply. "Maybe I could do a business degree."

"Oh, Liv." Lucas sits down next to me and puts his hand on top of mine. "That was six years ago, and I don't know, I feel like it might be too much for you."

"Why would you say that? You're a teacher; you should be encouraging me. Don't you try to inspire your students to continue learning?"

He smiles at me, but not his happy smile, not his sexy smile, but his patronizing smile. I hate it. I hate it so *damn* much. "If you applied right out of high school, sure. I think that would have been great, but now... you're older and with your family history, you know how your mom was..."

I glare at him. I hate when he talks down to me, assuming he knows me better than I know myself. "This has nothing to do with my mother! And why are you talking about me like I'm seventy years old? I'm only twenty-four; I'm not old!"

"Of course, of course," he quickly says. "I'm just saying I don't want you to be disappointed. I love you. I want you to be happy. I want to make you happy. Don't I try to give you the best life I can? We have a nice life, and I don't know why you'd want to change anything."

I don't say anything. This is the route he always takes when I bring up an idea he doesn't like or approve of, and I guess he's right. Maybe I'm not thinking clearly about this. He's worried about me, he wants to make me happy, let him make me happy.

And I've always liked hearing those words, but I have a stirring inside of me and it seems to be strengthening as time passes. I don't think I just want to be Mrs. Lucas Hanson. Sure that's part of who I am, but it isn't the complete package. The other part wants something just for myself, separate from Lucas. That's not wrong, is it? Why does he always seem so threatened when I suggest something for myself?

"Liv." He pushes the brochures even farther away from me and moves closer to me, kissing me. "You know I just want to take care of you and make you happy."

I used to believe him when he said those words, so why is it that now they are sounding false to my ears? Conflict rises inside me; there's so much I love about Lucas, yet he makes me so mad when he can't understand I need more in life, but those old connections and patterns always keep me with him, doing what he wants, even if I have different ideas. But if I keep doing this, I'll never grow and explore the areas that interest me. I don't want to be an old woman and regret the life I lived. I'm not giving up on this idea or many more; I only need to think about how I'm going to put them into action.

"Let's go out to dinner." I force a smile at him. "That will make me happy."

For now.

I wake up after midnight, restless and agitated, so I get out of bed with Lucas, put on my robe, and walk downstairs to get a glass of water. I change my mind when I reach the refrigerator and instead, I open the freezer and retrieve an ice cream sandwich from the bottom drawer where Lucas hides them.

I sit down and sink my teeth into the creamy vanilla ice cream between two rich chocolate cookies and think about our ridiculous dinner earlier this evening. Lucas avoided the topic of college like the plague. Instead, he praised me for decorating our home so beautifully, talked about our gym workouts and how happy I make him. He reminisced about our relationship and as I listened to everything he said, I realized how he speaks about everything in relation to him and how it affects him.

Why haven't I noticed this in the past? I always thought he was such a good listener. That's a big part of how I began to trust him in the beginning when he was only my soccer coach. He listened to me more than anyone had ever done in my life, I felt heard and seen, but now I see how he would cherry pick parts of those conversations to use to his advantage, specifically to gain my trust and admiration. He's the one who listened to me, so therefore, he is the only one I need. He could fulfill everything I would ever need. A trap that I walked into voluntarily and unknowingly until I was firmly entrenched within its invisible, but powerful, bars.

Lucas wants me to stay exactly the same. The same as I was at seventeen. In awe and dependent on him, hanging on his every word, thinking he was smarter than me since he's older than me.

As old as my father.

If I'd ever known him.

I've been thinking about my father lately. He left when I was around three years old, according to my mother. I have a vague recollection of him, dark hair and a nice laugh. I remember playing restaurant, or maybe it was a tea party, not exactly sure but I know food played a part in it because I remember asking what he would like to eat and preparing imaginary food. Mom got rid of any pictures we had of him, so the only memory I have is this foggy whisper of time spent with him without a real beginning or end. I've tried for years to try to clear my memory to really see his face, his mannerisms, anything that may define him as a person, but I've always been unsuccessful, just a floating haze of a man with dark hair and a nice laugh who fathered me and then left me.

I looked for him at my high school graduation. Doesn't every father want to see their child graduate from high school; even if they abandoned you, wouldn't they still feel a shred of pride that their child is accomplishing something in this world? I don't know why I bothered; my mother wasn't there either.

But Lucas was there. He took my picture. Brought me flowers. Told me he was proud of me. He made me feel like a star. He was the only one in the world who cared about me. He cared more about me than I cared about myself. He truly loves me like I love him, well maybe not as intensely as I love him. I don't think what Lucas feels for me is complicated. It's probably very simple to him and likely always has been so simplistic, but my feelings and understanding of those feelings are much more complicated. At seventeen I was oblivious to so much. My thoughts were very much black and white, right or wrong, probably common for most at that age, but now I see how much gray area comprises this journey of life. People make decisions for so many reasons, not necessarily the obvious reason. Even with the reasons presented to me at that time, I wouldn't have acknowledged them, but now the reasons are becoming real to me. Time changes not only your physical appearance, but also your mental appraisal.

I take another bite of ice cream sandwich. But I'm not a toy or a doll that stays the same with the same sweet smile painted on. I'm a woman who changes and has different ideas than when I was seventeen years old. What would happen as I age? When I turn forty, fifty years old?

Would Lucas still love me?

A sick feeling trickles through me as doubt sets in. How could he? I'm not sure if he really knows me, the real person inside. If I try to deviate from what he thinks I am he usually roadblocks it. He only sees my pretty outer coating, but what happens when that coating becomes cracked and lined with human experience? What if I change drastically in appearance, but I'm still the same person inside. Still a loving, vibrant, smart person, but would he see me? He's not perfect and I would love him always, no matter what may happen in life. But would he love me? Tears form in my eyes.

I don't know.

Would he even know me?

FOURTEEN

Olivia

It's Friday night and I stretch out on the sofa and scroll through my phone as Lucas watches some action movie I have already lost interest in. I prop up the pillow behind me and settle in, trying to get comfortable. I close my eyes, trying to forget about the letter I received in the mail today. It was addressed to Lucas, but curiosity overwhelmed me and I opened it. Now I'm sorry that I did because the contents of the letter are unsettling to say the least. I open my eyes again, unable to relax, then flick through Instagram and a text pops up. Natalie.

She wants to meet for lunch tomorrow.

> Sure
>
> Where and when?

The Mexican restaurant in the mall at one? I have a few errands to run first.

> OK, I'll be there.

I smile, staring at my phone. Natalie and I texted a couple times this week and now lunch tomorrow. That will be fun. Something to look forward to doing.

"Who are you texting?" Lucas asks, taking his attention away from the movie.

"Natalie."

He looks at me, a slight frown on his face. "Really?"

I meet his gaze. "Yes, really. I've talked to her a few times since the carnival." I neglect to mention going over to her house last Saturday. I don't think he'd like it, for some reason.

He's quiet for a few moments. "What did she want?"

"We're meeting for lunch tomorrow."

"Oh," is all he says.

"Why are you being weird?" I ask. "We don't have anything planned. You said you are going golfing again."

"Yeah, I know," he replies, reaching for my hand, intertwining his fingers with mine like that first time he kissed me so many years ago. "It just seems funny that you and Natalie have much to talk about."

"Oh, she's great, I really like her."

Lucas smiles. "Good. And what about Debbie? You two always have a good time together."

I raise my eyebrows at him. Debbie is his partner teacher in fourth grade. She's very nice and Lucas and I have joined her and her husband for dinner a couple of times, but that's it. Debbie is more Lucas's friend than mine. Anything I told her would go straight to him. I rather like that he's irritated by me making plans with Natalie, as long as he's not angry at me. I hate when he's angry at me.

"Debbie's nice, but we're not really friends, just friendly, but Natalie and I seem to click," I reply.

"Hmmm... that's nice," he says half-heartedly.

"Do you have a problem with me being friends with her?"

He clears his throat. "No, of course not."

I smile at my husband. "I think it's because she likes me more than you. She's not falling under the Lucas Hanson charm."

Now he laughs. "Oh, really? Am I that charming?"

The mood turns lighter, but I think I hit a nerve. Lucas is uncertain about Natalie.

And that makes me like her even more.

I arrive at the restaurant early and get a booth for us in the back of the busy restaurant. I text Natalie, telling her where I'm sitting, and she responds that she'll be there in five minutes.

I ask the waitress for a pitcher of water and two glasses. I like to drink a certain amount of water every day; the only exceptions are my green juice or protein shake and coffee in the morning and an occasional glass of wine in the evening. Lucas says water is the fountain of youth.

Natalie waves to me from across the restaurant and hurries over to me. She has a couple of shopping bags in her hands and a wide smile on her face.

"Hi, Olivia," she says, scooting into the seat. "Thanks for getting us a table."

"No problem," I reply. I point to the bags. "What did you get?"

"Oh, this week is color week in kindergarten and Emma needed something orange for Wednesday. I found a cute shirt for her."

"That's fun. Where's Emma today?"

"She's with her dad this weekend."

I nod. "Did everything work out with Candace last week?"

"Yes, it did. I took your advice, called Candace, and smoothed everything out. I'm glad I did it; things seem back to normal and that works for me."

"Good, I'm glad to hear that," I say, taking a sip of water.

THE INNOCENT WIFE

The waitress stops by with menus, tortilla chips and salsa.

Natalie pours water into her glass. "It's a relief. So how was your week?"

"Pretty good. I painted the living room this week. Light gray. It really brightens up the room; the old color was too dark and drab."

"Sounds nice." She looks over the menu. "I'm getting steak fajitas. What about you?"

"Grilled chicken salad."

We chat after we order and before we know it our food arrives.

"You know, I have an idea," Natalie says, taking a bite of her fajita.

"What?"

"Why don't you volunteer a couple days a week in my classroom, or Lucas's, if you prefer."

"Ohh... he wouldn't like it if I was there that often. I usually volunteer for special events or help the PTA organize activities."

"Okay, then if you volunteer in my room, Lucas wouldn't see you that often throughout his day." She looks at me and grins. "But why wouldn't he want to see you there? And the bigger question, who cares if he doesn't like it?"

"I guess." I smile and think about her suggestion. I'm sure I'd enjoy it and maybe I'm wrong. Lucas might like it; he always wants me to help out here and there. This will be a more regular volunteer position. Who knows, maybe if I'm at school more I may want to go to college to become a teacher. I considered it before, especially now after looking through my options; it may be the right choice for me. And she is right. Why do I always worry if Lucas will like it or not?

"I think it would be great," Natalie says. "Even if you just want to do afternoons. I think we would have such a great time working together."

"I'm liking the idea," I say. I take a bite of my salad, mulling over the thought. By the time I swallow the food, my mind is made up.

"Two days a week in the afternoon," I reply.

"How about three?" she counters.

I laugh. "You're quite the negotiator. Okay, three afternoons."

Look at that, I have a new job, sort of, but more importantly I have a new friend, which makes me the happiest of all.

Sunday night Lucas made plans for us to go out to dinner with his partner teacher, Debbie, and her husband, Mark.

"What time are we meeting them at the restaurant?" I ask him.

"Six thirty," he replies. "Why don't you wear that new dress I got you? The blue one?"

"Okay," I reply. "That's kind of low cut for dinner at the Seafood Shack though."

He put his arms around me and pulls me close to him, kissing me. He's been extremely affectionate since I went out to lunch with Natalie, and peppered me with questions last night about my conversation with her. I found it amusing how uneasy he felt about her. Or maybe it's because I'm spending time with someone other than him, either way a plus for me. "I want to show you off. You look so good in that dress."

I smile and kiss him back. I enjoy his attention when he's like this, like he used to be years ago, and this behavior still shows up from time to time. I love when it makes an appearance.

We hold each other and kiss for a few minutes, then I notice the time on the clock. I pull away from him.

"If we need to be at the restaurant by six thirty, we better hurry up and get ready."

. . .

The restaurant is one of those dark atmospheric places that you can barely read the menu or see the food, but it is intimate, and they have the best sangria and crabcakes.

"I bet we're all getting the same thing," Debbie says, trying to read the menu by dim candlelight. "Crabcakes?"

"Sounds good to me," Lucas says, closing the menu. He looks at me. "How about you?"

"Definitely crabcakes and some of that delicious sangria."

"Oh, that's so good here," Debbie agrees.

"I think we'll just stick with water," Lucas says, still looking at me. "You know it's the fountain of youth."

"Oh, Lucas, you and your fountain of youth. Water's great, but you and Olivia can splurge a bit. You're both very youthful looking." Debbie laughs.

"Debbie, let them order what they want," her husband, Mark, interjects.

"Well, he's not letting Olivia order what *she* wants," she says to her husband pointedly.

The waiter shows up before Mark has a chance to respond, and we place our orders.

"Any drinks?" the waiter asks.

"Sangria for me," Debbie says, shooting a look our way.

"Iced tea," says Mark.

The waiter looks at us.

"Water is fine for us," Lucas replies.

I smile, but I'm seething inside. Ridiculous fountain of youth.

Where did he even get that phrase?

FIFTEEN

Natalie

I pull up to Jake and Candace's house and park in the driveway. I put the car in park and look back to Emma sitting in the backseat, still reading her Curious George book.

"Ready to go see Daddy?" I ask. "Don't forget your backpack. You're sleeping over tonight."

"Got it," she replies, dropping her book onto the seat.

I smile and open the back door as she scurries out with her purple backpack. She runs up to the front door as Jake opens it and leaps into his open arms.

"There's my girl," Jake says, hugging her.

"Daddy," she giggles, then runs into the house.

I walk up and wave to Candace, who's standing inside. The smell of fresh baked cookies wafts out of the door. "Ooh, someone's baking," I remark.

Jake's eyes light up. "Yeah, Candace's making cookies and I'm eating them. Want one?"

I laugh. I love seeing him so happy; it is obvious he and Candace are a good fit, even if she's still cautious about me.

"No, I'm good. I have to get going or else I'll be late for my appointment."

"Okay, I'll send some home with Emma tomorrow," he says. "See you later."

"Bye." I wave and get back into my car.

He waves and goes back into the house. I pull out of the driveway and travel down the road through the development where they live, then turn left onto the main road. I turn up the music and glance at the time. Plenty of time to get to my eye doctor appointment. I can enjoy a leisurely drive and some good music on my way there.

It's nice to have some time to think. Things have been busy lately and I think I need to do something for myself soon. I've been toying with the idea of getting back into dance, maybe sign up for a class. I took ballet classes for years when I was younger and always loved the clarity and peacefulness I felt when dancing. I had a dream of being a famous ballet dancer as I'm sure most young girls do, though honestly, I wasn't that good, but still enjoyed it. Emma takes dance class and enjoys it. I make a mental note to look into some adult dance classes.

Such a beautiful fall day. The leaves are turning into brilliant hues of red and gold and I enjoy their shimmering colors in the crisp autumn air. I accelerate and glide along the empty road. I press the button to lower the window to allow some fresh air inside the car, inhaling its sweet scent. A loud noise comes from behind me, a strong roar coming out of nowhere. I look into the rearview mirror, seeing a flash of blue fly around me, then abruptly cut in front of me.

I slam on the brakes, my car spinning around. My head whips around as my car veers off the road, then cracks hard against something. My neck snaps back then forward into the ballooning air bag in front of me. My head aches as it descends into it and pain sears through the right side of my body.

My head falls forward and my eyes close.

. . .

My head is pounding. I try to open my eyes, but they are so heavy I can barely flutter them. It feels as if they are plastered shut. I moan and feel a hand on my arm and a soothing voice talking to me. I try to focus on the voice; it's familiar to me.

I concentrate on opening my eyes again and I get about halfway there, thin slits of light filter through, but they are so incredibly heavy.

"Hey, Nat." I hear Jake speaking. "You're okay."

"Mmmm..." I murmur. Finally, my eyes open and I stare at him, staring at me. "Where am I?"

"The hospital," he says, smiling at me. "You had a car accident and hit a tree. I'm glad you woke up."

I touch my head. "My head hurts."

"They did some scans and you're physically okay, just bruised, and sore. The doctors were waiting for you to wake up and see how you're doing cognitively. They'll keep you here tonight to monitor everything, then you can go home tomorrow," he says. "Do you remember what happened?"

I try to think; with effort, cloudy memories start to come through. "Um... I was driving and something flew around me, something blue, maybe a motorcycle? It ran me off the road. I guess into a tree."

My mind is foggy, but then the memory of it comes flooding back to me. Spinning, then hitting something and the pain, then I must have passed out. And now I'm here. Emma. Where's Emma?

"Where's Emma?" I sit up a bit, but lean back again because of the pain.

"With Candace."

I nod. "Good. Who would run me off the road?"

"I'm sorry, Nat," he says, holding my hand. I squeezed it. "I don't know."

I sigh and close my eyes.

Who indeed?

I settle in on the sofa after Olivia adjusts the pillows and snuggle under the soft chenille blanket, pulling it up to my chin. I snatch the TV remote from the coffee table.

"Okay, now you're all comfortable, find a movie and relax," Olivia says. "I'll get you some juice."

"No, I had enough, thanks, Olivia, you don't have to wait on me," I reply. "I appreciate it, but really you've done enough."

She smiles at me. "You're not getting rid of me that easy. I'm going to make you a pot of chicken rice soup, and you'll have some leftover chicken for sandwiches. Then you can have soup and a sandwich whenever you're hungry."

"Thank you so much. You're taking great care of me." I smile at her. "You're a good friend."

"You're welcome," she says quickly; a hint of tears shines in her eyes, then she hurries to the kitchen.

Jake brought me home yesterday. I'm bruised and sore, but otherwise fine. I just need to rest for a week before going back to work. Jake is keeping Emma at his house for the week, but they will come by after school to check on me. Initially, Emma wanted to stay with me to help me get better, which was so sweet, but we explained I needed to rest, and I'd be fine in a few days, which she accepted. She made sure to give me her special bear though to help me get better. Olivia stopped by last night and was back this morning. She's taking such good care of me. I think I'd feel so much worse if not for her friendship. I glance at my phone when it pings. A couple missed calls and texts from a friend at the previous school I worked at, but I don't feel like talking, so I ignore him, for now. I can reply later.

I find a movie and lean back into the pillows, getting more comfortable. I've been running the accident over in my mind all morning. Was it really an accident? Nobody witnessed what happened and other than the blue flash of movement I saw, I don't have any information, so it's doubtful we'll ever know the identity of the other driver.

It probably was just an accident, a reckless driver on the road the same time as me. I've been thinking about Theo too much lately and I'm feeling paranoid about everything, but accidents happen and that's the end of the story, I'm certain. Still, I can't help the anxious feeling of terror at the thought of what could have happened. I might so easily have left Emma without a mother. Even worse, what if she had been in the car too?

SIXTEEN

Olivia

I leave a sleepy but functioning Natalie just before the school day ends, as her ex will be bringing Emma round. Before going home, I stop at the grocery store. I want to bake some brownies tonight to take over to Natalie's house tomorrow. I know how much she loves chocolate and I'm sure some fresh baked brownies will make her smile. Then I grab a rotisserie chicken and a large ready-made salad at the deli for dinner and head home.

Lucas is already in by the time I get there, sitting at the kitchen table, looking through the mail. I walk through the door from the garage into the kitchen and kick it closed since my hands are full of grocery bags. He doesn't move to help me.

He only looks up from the mail, glaring at me.

"Where were you?" His voice is tense.

"I told you I was going over to Natalie's today."

He flings the mail on the table. "All day?"

I press my lips together. *He's in a mood.* "Not all day. I stopped at the grocery store too."

I rummage through the bags, placing the items on the table. Lucas eyes each item as I sit them down.

"What is all this? Sugar, baking cocoa, flour... what are you making?"

"Brownies to give to Natalie tomorrow. I got us dinner too." I put the chicken and salad on the table.

"Oh, great, supermarket chicken and salad." He sighs. "And you're going over to her house again? What is it with you and Natalie? It's like you're obsessed with her or something."

I drop the bag of flour on the table more forcefully than intended, and it slams with a heavy thud. I'm not going to do what he wants me to do like I usually do. I need to start standing up for myself. "What is wrong with you? She was in a car accident! She needs help right now."

"I'm sure she has family, and she has her ex-husband, right? Plenty of help. She doesn't need you at her beck and call."

"But I can be at yours?" I snap. "I'm so sick of your attitude right now, Lucas! So sick of it!"

He seems taken aback at my tone and confusion crosses his face for a moment. Then he stands up and glares at me again. "Then I'll go. I don't need to listen to your whining."

He grabs his keys and stalks out the door, slamming it behind him.

I gather the ingredients to make the brownies while tears sting my eyes. What kind of relationship is this? I tell myself I'm in love with him, but sometimes I think it's more of a fear of being by myself. Even if I do love him, I'm not happy with him. Isn't love supposed to make you happy?

SEVENTEEN

Him

I park my motorcycle along the narrow side road by the wooded area and take off my helmet. Sunlight trickles through the trees, shining off the blue paintwork and down over my face while a slight breeze ruffles my hair. A perfect autumn day.

I meant to scare Natalie a bit today, but I may have gone overboard. I never meant for her to crash into a tree. I only wanted to play a bit, scare her, make her uneasy and fearful, but not put her in the hospital. I didn't want to hurt Natalie, at least not today. Maybe not ever, if she makes the right decisions. Lately, though, she hasn't been very good at that.

I did the right thing though. I called 911 after she crashed, although only after I was a substantial distance away. No need to be involved in such a situation, but at least I called.

I'm not a complete monster.

EIGHTEEN

Natalie

About a week later, bruises mostly healed, and headache completely gone, I go back to school for the first time since the accident. I'm happy to get back into my normal routine and see my students again. And feeling surprisingly rested after the unplanned time off. Emma made me a welcome back to school card that she insists I hang up in my classroom. She colored it with purple, yellow, and red flowers and many, many hearts. I love it. I tack it up on the bulletin board next to my desk with her other artwork and that of my students, as well.

The door opens and Abby steps through with a pink bakery box and two tall coffee cups. The door squeaks shut.

"Yay, she's back!" Abby exclaims. "Coffee and doughnuts to celebrate!"

I smile. "You are the best. I hope there's a chocolate éclair in there."

"One for you and one for me." Abby sits one of the coffees on my desk and opens the box as I select my favorite doughnut, then take a bite.

"Oh, this is good," I say, then take a sip of coffee. "I needed this."

"I'm so happy you're feeling better." Abby laughs. "It wasn't the same around here without you."

"So how did everything go here? Anything new?" I ask, taking another bite of doughnut.

"Well, your sub was very nice; I was thrilled we got a sub even just for three days of the week; you know how that often goes," Abby says. She walks over to her table and drops her bag down on it, then opens her laptop. "Anyway, everything went well for the most part. I'm sure she left notes for you. Nothing too unusual. Although, there was one thing..."

"Yes?"

"Mrs. Dixon, that was your sub, and Haley, on the days she was here, went down to Mr. Hanson's room in the afternoons." Abby pauses. "I guess that was only two of the days the sub was here. Haley went down on her own the other day."

"Okay," I reply. "And?"

Abby sighs. "Nothing specific, but Haley stayed in his room after Mrs. Dixon would bring the students back here. She said Lucas requested Haley to stay and help him with a few things. Mrs. Dixon mentioned they were very... friendly."

"Overly friendly?"

"Nothing specific I guess, but you know how rumors fly around a school." Abby looks pointedly at me. "I'm sure you've noticed how he is around women. Well, I guess to be honest, everyone; he is very charming."

"I've noticed."

"He had a student teacher two years ago from a local college. She said he flirted with her, quite obviously when they were alone in the classroom, and it was a bit much. She told him to back off and he did, but she said he was incredibly persistent."

I take another bite of doughnut and nod. "He is persistent. Has he had any other issues like that in the past?"

"That's the only one I know about." Abby presses her lips together. "Now that I think about it, I remember there was something about one of the other teacher's daughters. She was young, probably eighteen, just graduated high school. I think it was a similar situation, him giving her a lot of attention. You know, attention a married man should be giving his wife."

I nod. "Good to know. Did anyone go to the principal about what happened?"

Abby shakes her head. "Not that I know of. This was a few years ago and we had a different principal, actually an old college buddy of Lucas's, so I don't know if anything would have happened if it was mentioned."

I nod, pondering the new information.

Maybe Lucas isn't as popular as I once thought.

"We're going to do the first two problems in your workbook, then go over them together. There is an example on the board, and you can always reread what we went over earlier," I say to the class. "Raise your hand if you have any questions."

Most of the students start to work on their problems. I give a reminder to the few that are staring at the wall or fiddling with their pencils, then walk to the back of the room to retrieve the water bottle from my school bag that sits on Lucas's back table.

He had to go to the office and talk to Andrea about one of his students, so I took over his class. I prefer being in here alone with the students; hopefully the matter in the office will take a substantial amount of time. I take another drink of water and walk over to his very organized desk.

He was always a neat freak. Everything in its specific place, even the stack of papers in the center of his desk and in the black inbox are in a particular order, I'm sure. Even years ago, when I would help him organize the equipment after the games, he was precise with where everything went, and his small coaching office was immaculate.

There's a coffee mug sitting to the right of the inbox, *Best Teacher Ever* emblazoned on the side. A black framed photo of Lucas and Olivia sits on the left of the desk. It was taken on a beach, the ocean behind them; he's dressed in a white button shirt and khaki shorts, she in a pretty aquamarine dress. A protein bar lies at the top of his desk, next to his dark blue Yeti water bottle. I don't know what I'm looking for, just being nosy, I suppose.

I glance at the photo again, not at Lucas, but Olivia. I appreciate her kindness when I was recovering from the accident; she went above and beyond to help me. She's such a compassionate person and I fear, if she stays with him, eventually Lucas will crush her.

The classroom door opens and Lucas strides in, briefly pausing to look at me staring at his desk. His eyes narrow.

"May I help you with something, Mrs. Amaryllis?" he asks; his eyebrows rise.

"No, I'm fine, Mr. Hanson," I reply, walking away from the desk. "Everything straightened out at the office?"

"Yes, of course." He walks over to his desk and takes a drink from his water bottle, his gaze still on me. "Feeling better?"

I nod, noting the agitation in his tone, although I'm not sure why my car accident would cause him irritation.

Unless he was the one who caused it? Where did that thought come from?

I chide myself for the ridiculous idea, and press my lips together for a moment before I can meet his gaze. "Yes, I'm feeling great. Olivia was such a help to me. She's a wonderful person."

His mouth smiles, but not his eyes. "She is wonderful. Well, I'm glad you're feeling better."

He takes another drink of water, sits it down and looks quizzically at me again, then walks to the front of the room.

Anger rises in me at his insincere comment. Everything about him is so deliberate, so well controlled and it infuriates me. When I was recovering from the accident I allowed my thoughts to go back to my days with Lucas, and as I think about it as an adult I realize how he must have planned every impromptu meeting and flirtation all leading one way. A well-planned grooming.

I bet you're glad I'm feeling better.

Even though I'm sure he doesn't recognize me, he definitely doesn't like me.

And the feeling is mutual.

NINETEEN

Natalie

I take out items from the dryer—shirts, pants, underwear—fold them, and place them into the laundry basket, eager to get Saturday morning chores finished. Then I walk upstairs, first to Emma's room, to put the freshly laundered clothes away. I always love putting her small, brightly colored clothing in their proper locations. I loved doing the same with her baby clothes. I'm still amazed that I'm responsible for a tiny little human, and I love that responsibility. All of it overwhelmed me in the beginning, but having Emma was truly the best thing that has ever happened to me in my life. A whoosh of love runs through me just thinking about her.

My thoughts travel back almost six years ago when I was only three months pregnant. Scared, terrified, and so unsure of my future. But certain of one thing: She would always be my baby, never his.

When I first met Theo, I sat alone at a bar, nursing a drink and a bruised ego at having been stood up by a no-show from a dating app. When Theo breezed in, I instantly clocked the good-looking man with dark blond hair, blue eyes, and a small scar above his right eyebrow. As soon as we started talking I was hooked. Theo was magnetic, exciting, unpredictable. Life felt like a whirlwind from the moment I met him and I was carried along in its grip.

He lived in an upscale neighborhood of Pittsburgh and lived life to the full. It was a stark contrast to my small apartment close to the school where I worked, and even smaller social network. I had never moved back home with my parents after college. Not after everything that had happened years ago. I barely spoke to them.

Theo begged me to move in with him and it was heaven for the first month or two, but when his possessiveness and anger started to dominate his personality and our lives, I felt confined like a rat in a trap. I sank further and further into the dark depths of his personality, always trying to please him, while losing myself. I couldn't be myself anymore; all of my actions revolved around how he would react. It was no way to live. Such a dark nonexistence. I didn't want to live with this sort of violence in my life, or the uncertainty of being with him. He was so volatile I never knew what to expect. Theo was a completely different person than who he presented to me in the first few months. He was a terrible person. And a criminal.

Then I found out I was pregnant.

I had to get out.

I'd kept in touch with Jake, less frequently once I got together with Theo, but enough that he was willing to help me get out when I called, scared and alone, from a payphone. But our original plan changed with the heavy knock of a policeman on the apartment door. Theo had been arrested.

A twenty-one-year-old girl had been murdered at a club. She had been seen with Theo earlier in the evening, but he denied everything. Yes, he'd been speaking to her in the club briefly, but then went home to me. I was his alibi.

Theo was home with me that night, of course—I had the black eye to prove it—but this was my chance. I testified against him. I told the court he never came home that night. I lied under oath to save myself and my unborn child. And if I had the choice, I'd do it again.

Our freedom came at a price, however. Having to lie to my daughter every day about who her father is. Terrifying nightmares where he gets out sooner than he should and comes after me for the lie. But all of it only makes me more sure that I've done the right thing, that I have to keep Emma safe and protected. I have to keep Theo out of her life, and she can't ever know he even exists. I know he would only destroy her, like he tried to do to me.

Later that evening, I'm putting on my pajamas when the doorbell rings. I glance at the clock. Nine forty-five. Who would that be? I look at my phone to see if anyone texted that they were stopping over. Nothing.

I walk over to Emma's room, who is at a sleepover at Becky's house, and peek out her window to the driveway below. Only my car is parked in the driveway.

I pad downstairs and approach the front door. I look out the peephole but see no one. I hesitate to open the door and instead stand quietly by it, listening for any movement by the front door. I was upstairs for several minutes; maybe the person already left.

I stand there for several more minutes, while the world is silent around me. Why am I scared to open the door? I chalk it up to my thoughts about Theo, but he's still in jail.

Isn't he?

Yes. He was sentenced to twenty years, but eligible for parole after ten. I still have a few years without worry. Even then, he has no way of knowing my location.

I'm being paranoid. I take a breath and open the door just to be certain there's no one there. A florist's box sits on the welcome mat. A tall vase of red roses sits inside with a little white envelope in the center.

I smile, cast a quick glance around, but see nothing unusual. Just a flower delivery, late, but it's a Saturday; they are probably busy. I wonder who sent them?

I lift the roses up, lock the door and place them on the kitchen table. I open the little white envelope and pull out the small card inside.

I read the typed message.

```
Natalie, Guess Who?
```

TWENTY

Natalie

I drop the card on the table and stare at the flowers. The box the vase is contained in doesn't have a florist's name on it, just plain white cardboard. No name on the card either, so I assume someone picked this up at Target or a grocery store. Coldness inches up my spine. This means someone personally delivered the bouquet.

I stare at the beautiful full red blooms and imagine who placed them at my doorstep.

Theo?

Lucas? Did he recognize me after all?

I run upstairs back to Emma's room, remembering how she asked about the man staring at the house. She hasn't mentioned him again, but could it be connected to the flower delivery? Is someone watching us? The thought of someone keeping track of our comings and goings unnerves me. Goosebumps form on my arms and my stomach lurches.

I pull open the curtains and survey the surroundings. The moon is partially obscured, allowing a few ripples of moonlight to filter through. Nothing is unusual in our driveway or the front yard. I peer across the road paying particular attention to the dark recesses of the building.

A large bush sits to the left of the walker door, on the right side of the building, but it seems wider than normal. I stare harder.

Is someone standing behind the bush?

Watching our house?

I stare at it for a full fifteen minutes, my gaze never wavering, and while it still appears wider than normal there is no movement. Maybe my mind is only playing games and there is nobody standing there. I shrink away from the window and sit on Emma's bed.

Could it be Lucas? Did he figure out who I am? I know it's a gamble to ask Olivia to volunteer during the same hours Haley is there, but it is the best idea I have to keep an eye on Lucas's interaction with Haley. But even if he knows who I am, what is the point of sending me flowers with a strange note? Things didn't end well with us, but that was twenty years ago.

I think again about the note, *Guess Who*. Two men in my life have given me roses before: Lucas and Theo. If the delivery is a threat from either of them, what message would they be trying to send me? Lucas would want me to back off from Olivia, and Theo would want his money back and—my heart sinks.

Emma.

He would want *my* Emma.

I try to fall asleep but end up just tossing and turning. Finally, I get up at one. I walk over to Emma's room again and open the curtain. I stare over at the bush again and this time it looks narrower than it had earlier. I don't think it's my imagination. I go back to my bedroom to retrieve my phone and take a picture of the bush. If it seems wider again, I'll take another picture and compare the two.

I walk out of the bedroom and into the bathroom, splashing water onto my face, and take my time drying it off with the towel. I rather hope it is Lucas who sent the roses. I can deal with him. While he hurt me in the past, those emotional ties have long been severed and I can manage him.

But Theo?

He terrifies me.

Could he have been released early? I go back to my bedroom, pick up my phone, and start searching. Pennsylvania has a statewide automated Victim Info and Notification System to search to see if a prisoner has been released. I type in Theo's name, but "No Results Found" pops up. It says it could be a result of the facility being offline so I could try searching later.

The week of his trial, Theo had been at his partner Bobby's house. Organizing financials, he said, which meant hiding cash. The leather bag in the closet was the only cash he kept. He said he still needed some cash on hand and there wasn't any law prohibiting him from having it. I guess he forgot about the law prohibiting stealing it. He assumed the trial would go his way since I was his alibi; an elementary school teacher with a spotless record is a perfect alibi witness, right?

He didn't know the prosecutor had spoken to me at school, nor that I would testify that he was not at home. I had to do it; it was my only chance to be free of him.

I would lie to save myself and my baby, from him.

I tried not to look at him in court on the day I testified but felt his glare at me. Felt his anger and disbelief. I'd shocked him; he never saw me turning on him like that. He thought I'd listen to whatever he told me to do, and the funny thing is that he wanted me to tell the truth—for once truth was on his side—but I turned the tables on him. I revealed my true self to him that day. I would not take any more of his torment; I was done with him. And because I was such an upstanding citizen, an excellent witness, the court believed every word I said. My testimony gave Theo a one-way ticket to a jail cell.

Jake picked me up at the courthouse that day. He was staying at a nearby hotel where I had dropped off my suitcase, containing clothes, personal items, and the leather bag inside, and we traveled across the state to his home in the suburbs of Philadelphia. I couldn't go back to the apartment. I knew Bobby would be trouble for me. I married Jake and became Mrs. Amaryllis. My new life began.

I know I don't have to worry about Bobby at least. He was killed during a bank robbery just outside of Pittsburgh about a month later. He wasn't the sharpest pencil in the box and relied on Theo as the brains of their operations. Without Theo to mastermind the heist, he had gotten sloppy, and he paid for his carelessness with his life.

I lie back in bed and stay there until the sun starts to rise, long fingers of sunshine nipping through my curtains. I pull on my robe and walk downstairs to the kitchen, staring at the flowers again. They are objectively beautiful, nothing unusual about them, except the mysterious card which still lies on the table. I should throw them out, but I'll wait until a bit later. I busy myself making coffee and a cheese omelet.

I'm eating my breakfast, the clock slowly ticking behind me, eight o'clock in the morning, a full day ahead of me and I'm already exhausted. A text pops up on my phone from a number I don't recognize. It's not in my contacts.

> Did you like the roses?

I stare at the words.
It must be Lucas. How would Theo have this number?
Three dots appear. The person is still typing.

> Sorry it was a bit late when I dropped them off. I was hoping you'd be home but there was no answer.

I continue to stare at my phone. This doesn't sound like something Lucas or Theo would say.

I grab my phone and type,

> Who is this?

> 😄

> Sorry, I got a new phone last week and had to change my number because of some issues. I guess we haven't texted since. This is Ryan.

Relief sweeps through me and I laugh out loud at how much I'd worked myself up last night. Ryan. Ryan gave me the flowers. Suddenly I understand the message on the card.

I worked with Ryan at my old school; he is a second-grade teacher there, and he helped me move some of my things into my new place. I had five students on my caseload in his class, so we saw each other quite a bit. On Fridays, the class got to choose a game to play for the last half hour and his class always chose the Guess Who? game. It was a running joke between the two of us every Friday. Ryan is a nice guy and he'd expressed interest in going on a date with me after my divorce from Jake. As much as I like him, though, I'm not interested in dating. Friendship is as much as I can handle right now.

> Ryan!! You had me wondering about those roses. They are beautiful. Thank you!!

> Oh, sorry. I thought you'd know it was me by the message. I should have signed the card.

I smile.

> No worries. How are you?

> Pretty good. I heard you were in an accident. Are you okay?

Oh, I forgot he had called and texted me a few times and I never answered. I feel bad; he's such a nice guy.

> I'm so sorry I didn't answer your calls and texts. Things have been crazy lately. Yes, I'm doing very well. It was a minor accident.

> Great, glad to hear it. Hey, can I call you? Is this a good time to talk?

> Sure.

My phone rings a few seconds later and I end up chatting with Ryan for the next half an hour. School gossip, about my new job, about the new puppy he got two weeks ago. A really great conversation. Then things go quiet for a minute.

"I hope I wasn't over the line with the roses, especially red." Ryan laughs nervously on the other end of the phone. "I remembered you said once that red roses were your favorite because they were so vibrant. That's why I got them, but afterwards I thought it may have been a bit much."

I smile, enjoying his hesitancy and honesty. And the fact that he remembered me saying that impresses me. "No, not at all. I love the flowers and the thought behind them. You're very thoughtful."

"Oh, good." He laughs good-naturedly.

"I'm sorry to cut this short, but Jake is dropping Emma off in an hour and I wanted to take a quick shower before she gets home," I say.

"Sure, it was great talking to you," he replies.

"I really enjoyed it too and thanks again for the flowers."

"Of course. Just a little something to celebrate your new job." Ryan pauses. "Would you like to go out to dinner sometime?"

"Just as friends?" I ask. "That's all I'm interested in right now."

"I know," he says. "Just as friends. I miss seeing you every day."

I smile. I like Ryan a lot. "I miss you too. Thanks for understanding."

"Well, I'm lucky to have you as a friend," he replies, a slight tease in his voice.

"I think I'm the lucky one," I say, still grinning. "Okay, I really have to go. Bye."

"Bye, Natalie."

I click off the phone and sit for a few moments before going up to the shower. A wide smile crosses my face now when I look at the red roses sitting on the table.

What a nice surprise.

TWENTY-ONE

Olivia

I smooth a few flyaways in my hair, apply a hint of lipstick, and stand back to look at myself in the mirror. Black pants, a silky black and white striped blouse, and cute black sandals. Small gold hoop earrings. Ready for my first day in Natalie's classroom. My phone, sitting on the bathroom vanity next to my makeup bag, beeps and I pick it up staring at the sender.

It's her.

Again.

I don't want to talk to her now. I don't want to even think about everything she's told me. I place the phone down, trying to push the intruding thoughts out of my mind.

Lucas walks into the bathroom wearing his khaki dress pants but no shirt. He grabs his deodorant body spray and applies it. He shakes his head.

"Why are you getting ready now? You're only coming in the afternoon," he grumbles. "I'm not even ready yet."

"I take longer to get ready than you, plus I'm going in early, probably around ten thirty."

"You're still getting ready ridiculously early. What's the big deal anyway? You've volunteered at school before *Natalie* got here."

I look at him, not liking how he emphasized her name, as if he doesn't like her.

"What's your problem with Natalie?" I ask. "You're so weird about her."

"I am not!" he retorts, tossing his deodorant back into the closet. "But you think she knows everything. She suggests volunteering three days a week at school, and you say yes, without even asking me!"

"*Asking you?*" I snap, surprising myself. "I don't need to ask you to do anything."

"That's not what I meant. I mean without talking to me." His voice softens. "You know I like to take care of you. I want you to be happy."

I soften too and give him a hug. He draws me close. "I know you do," I whisper to him. "This is going to make me happy."

He sighs and pulls away. "Okay, then I guess I'll see you in a couple hours."

He kisses me and goes to put on his shirt.

I know Lucas wants to take care of me and it's part of what drew me to him. Nobody takes care of me like he does, certainly not my parents. I think we're different than most married couples who view each other as partners. Of course, Lucas loves me, but I don't think he's ever seen me as an equal partner, but more of a little girl he takes care of. When I think about it like that it sounds so... disturbing. I try not to think about it because it bothers me.

I look into the mirror and reapply the lipstick Lucas smudged, pushing the thoughts away.

. . .

I walk with Natalie, Haley, and four students down the hall to Natalie's classroom. Natalie will help the students with their independent work and then Haley and I will work on flash card skills when they are finished.

"Oh!" Haley exclaims. "I forgot my folder in Mr. Hanson's room. I'll go get it."

Natalie looks at me. "Would you mind getting it? I want Haley to help with the students."

"Sure," I say. "No problem."

I turn around and head back to Lucas's room. I open the door and he's already holding the folder with a big smile on his face, which lessens slightly when he sees me.

Is he disappointed I'm not Haley?

"Haley forgot her notebook," I say as he hands it to me.

"I know, I found it." He is still smiling. "How is your day going?"

"Good." I turn away. "I'll tell you about it at dinner."

Lucas nods as I walk out the door. I stare at Haley's folder, her name written across it in big puffy letters and a few little smiley faces doodled on the front cover. I peek inside and see a few notes and in the lower right-hand corner of the notebook a cluster of little hearts. Inside one a messy scribbled name. I squint at it. Then again. I could swear it says Lucas. I remember writing the same in my notebook when I was about her age. An old worry resurfaces inside me. Not again.

Maybe it's her boyfriend's name.

Or maybe it's my husband.

TWENTY-TWO

Natalie

Olivia seems a bit off when she comes back to the classroom after retrieving Haley's notebook. I finish with my small group and the students do flashcards with the two women. Anna comes in to go over her behavior chart for the day, and I check to make sure she has all her homework in her take-home folder. I add an envelope addressed to her parents with the Individualized Education Program invitation to our meeting next week. My list of IEPs is stacking up. I'll be up late several nights finishing up all the paperwork after Emma goes to bed.

Before I know it, the day is over, and Haley says goodbye and leaves. Olivia is lingering by the back table, gathering her flash cards. This morning, she was so full of enthusiasm, but now she appears deflated. Maybe she's just tired; it has been a busy day.

"How was your first day?" I ask.

"Good," she says, a bit absentminded. "Is Haley here every day?"

"No, just Wednesday, Thursday, Friday in the afternoons," I reply. "Same as you."

She nods. "Oh, that's good, I'm glad we have the same schedule; it probably works out well for you too. Well, I'm going to head out. I'll see you tomorrow."

"I'll be here!" I reply cheerfully. "I have to go to bus duty now. Have a good evening."

"You too," she says as I walk out the door, heading to the bus door by the office.

Did Olivia notice something already between Haley and Lucas? I want to ask her so badly, but that would be crossing the line. I feel good about having her here to keep Lucas in check. I'm glad I asked her to come in. Nothing is going to get past us. Lucas has two sets of eyes on him when it involves Haley. I'm so happy to have Haley in my classroom, and I feel responsible for keeping her safe. She really seems to enjoy working with the students and has that extra patience needed to work with students who have disabilities and need variations. I'm excited for her and her future. I see my younger self in her and I'll do everything I can to help her reach her goals. It's important to have older people in your life guide you along a path you want to take in your education or career. Despite my troubles with my parents, I'm grateful for them helping me with the college process when I told them I wanted to be a teacher. Life can be overwhelming when you're younger and having a seasoned person with you for questions or guidance is invaluable.

Surprisingly, the buses are all on time today, so bus duty goes quickly. I gather my bags from my classroom and go to get Emma at the walker door where she waits with her friend Becky.

"Bye!" her friend calls when I arrive at the door. She hurries away with her older sister.

"Have a good evening, Mrs. Stamos!" I say to the para who

is usually on walker duty. She works in Mr. Troutman's learning support classroom and is always so friendly to everyone.

"You too, Mrs. Amaryllis!" she calls, going back inside the building.

"Guess what, Mommy?" Emma asks, grabbing my hand.

"What?"

"Becky calls her mom, Mom, not Mommy," she says, her eyes wide. "Do you think I should too? I don't want to be a baby."

I shake my head. "You can use either one. If you want to, you could call me Mom at school to feel more grownup and Mommy at home," I suggest. "It's up to you."

"Yes!" She claps her hands. "I like that."

We walk home, trail up the driveway and approach the front door. As we near the door, we notice something. A medium-size bright pink box with a white ribbon on top sits on the welcome mat. Another surprise?

"Mommy!" Emma runs to it.

"Wait, Emma..."

It is no use. She lifts the lid and squeals when she sees the item inside. A limited-edition Barbie she's been talking about lately. There is a little card on the lid.

To Emma,
Enjoy your Barbie!

"I love it!" she exclaims. "Dad got it for me!"

"Let me look at it." She hands me the box. A typical Barbie box containing her special Barbie. The card was typed. I look inside the gift box. Empty.

Ryan? Jake? I don't think Ryan would leave a Barbie for Emma. Jake, maybe, but it's still odd. He would give her a gift when he saw her, not leave it on the front porch. I give the doll back to her and grab the box to take it inside with us.

Once inside, I lock the door and turn the deadbolt.

TWENTY-THREE

Olivia

I thought about that stupid heart in Haley's notebook all night and the way Lucas's smile dimmed when I walked into the room instead of her. Is my imagination in overdrive? It's probably nothing; maybe I misread the heart—the handwriting was messy. These same questions kept churning around in my mind and it all came back to the same question: Could there be something going on between them? It isn't out of the question. I was barely seventeen when my relationship with him started. Lucas is very persistent when he sees something he wants, or in this case, someone.

Does Natalie suspect something? Maybe that's why she suggested that I volunteer at the school more. I'm glad I'm there the same time as Haley. I'm going to be watching Lucas like a hawk. But I shouldn't have to watch him. I should be able to trust my husband.

But...

I don't want to think about this anymore.

Lucas crawls into bed with me, his arms around me, kissing

my neck. He pulls me closer to him. "Mmmm... you feel so good."

I don't respond.

"Liv, what's wrong," he asks.

"Did you like seeing me at school today?" I roll over to face him.

"Of course I did," he says, kissing me. "I always love seeing you."

"Do you?"

He grins. "Yes, I always love seeing you, every single part of you."

He always says what I want to hear, and I hope it is honest and true, although this line is obviously just so we have sex. Why am I feeling so conflicted about him lately? My feelings are complicated and confusing, not simple and straightforward as they once were, but I'm questioning different aspects now, when before I accepted everything.

"I love you," he tells me, continuing to kiss me, his hands moving down my body. "You're my girl."

I sigh, pushing the confusing thoughts aside, my body responding to him like always. "I love you too."

On Friday I'm standing in the office waiting to talk to Mindy, the school secretary, about the copier in the faculty room that I just jammed while copying packets for Natalie. I've had issues with the copier in the past and only on a rare occasion can find the correct area where the paper is jammed. Mindy is the only one with the magic touch to fix it. I tried, but only got a few pieces of paper out of the machine and black, inky hands.

Natalie is in the mail room off to the right side of the office. Lucas comes into the office and winks at me.

"I'm waiting for Mindy. Copier issues."

"Oh, yeah, she's the only one who can fix it." He walks to the mail room. "Better check my mailbox."

I watch him walk into the small room, but Natalie's body language captures my attention as he enters the space. Lucas turns away from her facing his mailbox and takes a few envelopes out. Natalie looks at him, her body rigid; an expression of disgust crosses her face, then disappears. In that instant she appears to hate him.

Why?

Why would she hate my husband?

She barely knows him.

Natalie is finishing up with her math group and the students head back to Lucas's classroom. Haley is sitting at the front table with her and I'm putting my activity packets together, thankfully saved from the copier's clutches by Mindy.

"Great group," Natalie says. "You explained number four very well to Sam. That one was really difficult for him."

"Thanks, it feels so good when they understand it. I love it." Haley beams. "I feel like I'm getting to know the strengths of each student and where they struggle. I think that's so helpful when you're trying to help them understand something."

"Oh, definitely."

"Oh." Haley stands up, looking around. "I left my sweatshirt in Mr. Hanson's room. I'll stop by and pick it up and then head out."

"Um..." Natalie says. "I'll get it. I have to go down anyway and talk to Lucas."

"No," Haley says. "I'll pick it up on my way out. You don't have to bother."

"Oh, no bother." Natalie stands up. "Let's walk down together."

Haley looks at her oddly. "Really, Mrs. Amaryllis, I'm fine doing it myself."

"Of course you are," Natalie says, breezily, ignoring her obvious attempts to avoid being accompanied to his room. "Okay, I'll be back soon, Olivia."

"Okay, bye, Haley," I say.

"Bye," she replies, giving me a quick wave as she follows Natalie out the door.

What a strange day, first the bizarre behavior in the mailroom; I cannot get the look on Natalie's face out of my mind when she saw Lucas next to her. Unnerving because I've never noticed anyone else react to him in that fashion, except me. But I know Lucas; I know that he's not as perfect as his outer appearance. Everyone else admires him though, sees him as friendly, handsome, and charming, someone they want to be around, talk to, joke with. As he often says, he's the life of the party. Not Natalie, though, and working at school for these couple of days with the two of them has accentuated the oddness between them. He's so irritated about her and doesn't like when I spend time with her. Both of their behavior is a bit odd. Now Natalie is practically running out of the door to go with Haley to Lucas's room.

Those puffy hearts drawn on Haley's notebook with the name scribbled inside spring into my mind. I can't stop thinking about those *damn* hearts. And the look of absolute disgust I saw on Natalie's face in the office mailroom toward my husband.

Why is Natalie acting so strange today?

Especially with anything relating to Lucas.

TWENTY-FOUR

Natalie

"Okay, go brush your teeth and pick out a book to read before bed," I tell Emma, helping her put on her pajamas. After a busy Friday, it's nice to wind down and relax.

"Curious George," she says, running into the bathroom. I follow her and make sure she takes enough time to brush. She rinses her mouth and smiles at me. My heart fills. I love this girl.

We snuggle into her bed to read her favorite Curious George book. George is making pancakes in this book and lots of silly things happen, of course. The new Barbie is lying next to her bed. I stare at it a moment.

"You're taking your Barbie to bed with you tonight," I remark.

She smooths the doll's long blond hair. "She's pretty. Dad gave her to me."

I smile; I guess we're losing Mommy and Daddy and becoming Mom and Dad, although I'm not sure why she says that Dad gave it to her, since I asked Jake and he said he didn't leave it. I asked her earlier about it and she said she told Jake that she wanted this particular Barbie, so I guess that's why she thinks he bought it for her.

"She is pretty, like you," I whisper to her. "You are very smart too."

"I know how to write my name and I read books too!"

"Yes, you do." I kiss her forehead. I continue to read the book, and it doesn't take long until her eyes fall shut and she's asleep.

I sit in the quiet and just enjoy watching her sleep. My relationship with Theo was a disaster, but it gave me Emma and for that I will always be grateful.

I get up and go to my bedroom. The house is a bit chilly, so I grab my robe and wrap it around me, then go downstairs, get my school laptop from my bag, and settle in on the sofa. I have two IEPs to write before Monday meetings, so I better start working.

I flick the TV on but keep the volume low. An old popular sitcom is on; I'm not really watching it, I just want the background noise as I type.

I work for about an hour and my mind wanders. Mostly to Haley. I must think of another way to talk to her. I can tell I'm annoying her and when I was talking about professional behavior with colleagues, she looked at me like I was losing my mind. I know I sound like some old lady lecturing her and that isn't going to build trust between us. But I'm sure something is up. Why is she suddenly leaving all her stuff in Lucas's room? Every day it seems she "forgets" something. I know something is off. Nobody forgets things that often.

I thought things would be better having Olivia there. I made a point of telling Haley she was Lucas's wife. Again, I must try another tactic because I know Haley thinks I'm a bit strange. At least tomorrow we have some testing to do, so we'll be staying in my classroom. Less time in Lucas's room the better.

What if I'm only obsessing about Lucas and Haley because of my past with him? I don't think I am though. I know how he creates this little world with just the two of you and how he tells you to keep it a secret because nobody else would understand. It infuriates me so much that he still plays these stupid games!

I continue to type but my mind is still on Haley. Why am I so interested in this thing between her and Lucas? Whatever it is, I can't get it out of my mind. Is it because Haley reminds me so much of myself at that age? Maybe. I know how he destroyed me, and I don't want him doing the same thing to her. He preys on vulnerability, and he's good at pretending to be a kind, caring person who always is there to listen to you. But that's not who he is though, because someone who truly cares about you would never do what he did to me. I wonder about Olivia too. She has more of a timid personality, but I see fire in her too. I think flames of that fire are starting to erupt in her, but she has trouble expressing herself honestly, probably because she's been molded by Lucas for years.

She was acting odd today. Distant, unlike herself, and even more reserved than normal. I hope it isn't something I did. My guess is it's something about Lucas.

Sometimes I think about how lucky I am that my relationship with Lucas dissolved, although it was heartbreaking and changed me significantly as a person. But at least I have my own identity. I feel like Olivia struggles with that, always wanting to please Lucas. He has that kind of power over you, making you think he's taking care of you, loving you, when all he's doing is controlling you. Being married to him must be difficult.

Olivia never had a chance to become her own person and I feel like she's searching for her place in the world besides being Lucas's wife. Maybe I can help her with that by being her friend and giving her the space to realize who she wants to be, not who Lucas tells her to be.

I haven't had one decent, long-lasting relationship in my life, and I think it all stems from my time with Lucas. That's one big reason I'm not dating, or even have the desire to date. I seem to attract the wrong men, and I've wasted too much of my life on them.

A text pops up on my phone. I glance at it. Ryan.

> Exciting Friday night? I'm grading math tests 😩

I smile and type.

> I'm working on IEPs

> LOL

> Hey, did you leave another gift at my front door the other day? Not the flowers. A pink gift box.

> No, only the roses.

Three dots.

I wait, but no message appears. Finally, one pops up.

> You must have a lot of admirers.

I laugh.

> No, it was a Barbie for Emma.

> Ha ha, hey, are you interested in dinner tomorrow?

Ryan is persistent, I'll give him that. But I did agree to dinner sometime.

> I'm busy this weekend I'm afraid. Next weekend?

> Sure! Have fun with your IEPs.

I press to like his text and sit my phone back on the coffee table. A smile spreads across my face. I may like Ryan a bit more than I admit, but I can't entertain the idea of anything more than friendship at this point. Although, I must admit I do desire to have a stable relationship sometime in my life. I feel like if something is right it will happen slowly and easily, not quickly, and it's a good thing I'm not in a rush. Then another thought pops into my mind.

Who did leave that Barbie for Emma?

Candace crosses my mind. After our phone conversation we spoke a few times and there's still a lingering awkwardness between us. I'm the only one who notices, and Candace of course. Jake thinks everything is fine. But if it was Candace, why do it in such a strange way, just to mess with me?

Things were odd between Candace and me in the beginning when she and Jake got together, but I always thought that was because she didn't know the whole story of our marriage and how it never was a real marriage, romantically speaking, simply a close friendship. And I could completely understand her feelings, but Jake and I had a discussion with her, told her the basics of everything and I thought she and I were good. Then, suddenly, she starts being standoffish with me and I have no idea why it happened. I want everyone get along and I know Jake wants the same thing as me.

Another text pops up.

Ryan, again? I look at the screen.

Nope, Olivia.

> What are you doing?

> Writing IEPs. You?

> Nothing much. Lucas went out with some friends from college tonight.

> Why didn't you go?

> I don't know. I don't like his friends.

I sigh. I really wanted to finish my paperwork, but she sounds lonely.

> Come over. I'll make some tea.

> OK, thanks, be there soon.

I lay the phone down again, finish typing the paragraph I'm working on and go to put the kettle on. She jumped at the invitation, I wonder if she has something else to tell me; maybe something happened at school, or maybe she is just lonely.

Olivia shows up a few minutes later and walks in when I open my front door. A gale of wind gushes in behind her, blowing my hair back. She has the hood up on her sweatshirt and raindrops in her hair.

"Raining?" I ask.

"Yeah, it just started," she says, pulling the hood down.

"The tea will soon be ready," I say. I open the pantry door to retrieve a pack of cookies. "I think we need a few treats."

"No, just tea for me."

"Just one?"

"No, Lucas doesn't like if I eat sweets; they're only for special occasions," she replies. "He doesn't eat them either."

I raise my eyebrows. "Really?" Does Lucas control every aspect of her life? She won't eat a cookie because of his instructions. *Ugh.* How suffocating it must be to be married to him.

She shrugs.

The kettle whistle goes, I prepare our mugs of tea, and we head to the living room.

Olivia looks at the laptop on the coffee table. "Am I keeping you from your work?"

"Nah, I needed a break." I settle in on the couch and open the cookies. Lucas doesn't control my dessert intake. I take two. "Why didn't you go out with Lucas and his friends tonight?"

"I always feel strange with them. All of his friends and their wives went to college and have careers." She sighs. "I don't fit in with them. It's not that they're not pleasant to me, but I feel like an outsider to all their conversations. Plus, they're twenty years older than me."

"So is Lucas," I remark.

"Yeah." She sips her tea. "I want to tell you something."

I meet her gaze. "What?"

"I think Haley may have a crush on Lucas. I feel dumb bringing this up, but I can't stop thinking about it. When I picked up her folder the other day, I saw a couple hearts drawn and one had Lucas's name inside," she says. "I mean, maybe she has a boyfriend named Lucas that I don't know about. Has she talked about a boyfriend?"

"Not that I know of."

"So, she probably has a crush on Lucas."

"Hmmm... yes, that's possible," I reply. This is evidence that even if nothing is going on, Haley is thinking about it.

"There's something about Lucas you don't know," she says, hesitantly.

"Tell me," I say, even though I know what she's going to say.

"I was sixteen when I met Lucas. He was my soccer coach." She pauses. "And we were in a relationship just after my seventeenth birthday."

I nod. I bet he brought her red roses for her birthday, just as he did for my fifteenth. He followed the exact same pattern of behavior to seduce her as he did me. I wonder how many other girls there have been.

"And you're worried he's going to turn his attention to Haley?"

"I don't want to think it, but it's possible if he knows she's interested in him."

"You think he would cheat on you?"

Tears form in her eyes. "I don't know. You don't know how Lucas is, how seductive he can be when he wants something."

My heart aches for her. The uncertainty and anguish she is feeling covers her face. I move closer to her and wrap my arms around her. Truth is I do know how Lucas is, unfortunately. I wonder if I should tell her about my past with Lucas. I ponder the thought for a few moments, but I don't think it's the right time.

"I should be able to trust my husband," she whispers. "I shouldn't feel threatened by a sixteen-year-old girl."

"Yes, you should. You know Lucas is the problem, not Haley."

She wipes her tears away. "I know. He never stopped liking teenage girls."

I nod. "You don't have to stay with him you know."

She looks thoughtful. "I always thought I loved him so much, but lately..."

"What?"

She sighs. "I wonder if I'm just scared to not be with him, not scared of him, but scared to be on my own."

I hug her again.

TWENTY-FIVE

Olivia

I close Natalie's front door, but I don't walk to my car yet. Instead, I sit on the top porch step, listening to the rain softly pattering around me, enjoying its soothing sound. I'm glad I opened up to Natalie. I trust her and I need someone to talk to about this. Lucas did go out with his friends tonight, but he's been out three nights this week all with varying excuses. I thought Natalie would be surprised by my revelation, but she wasn't fazed at all. It was as if she'd already known, but how could she?

He hasn't disappeared like this for years, not since his mother was sick; his excuse then was that he had so many extra responsibilities, which I never pressed him on and I don't know why not.

I look over to the side of the porch by Natalie's kitchen window. A green gum wrapper lies there. I move over and pick it up. It's Lucas's favorite type of gum. I finger the wrapper in my hands. Was this here when I arrived earlier? I shove it into my sweatshirt pocket.

A cool breeze pushes the rain onto me even though I'm still standing on the covered porch. I pull my hood up and run off the porch to my car. My phone buzzes. I pull it out of my pocket.

Her again.

I quickly read the text, but I don't answer. I can't believe she's texting me this late. I never should have made contact after receiving the letter, but her cell number was on it; I had to know more about the situation. I still haven't told Lucas about the letter. I told her I don't believe her, but she insists that what she's telling me is true.

What if it is?

I put the phone back into my pocket and sit in silence for a few more minutes. Then it beeps again. I pull my phone out.

Lucas.

> Where are you?

I stare at the message. I don't know if I want to answer.

> Olivia?
>
> You better answer me.

A few minutes pass.

> Answer me OLIVIA!

I toss the phone on the passenger seat.

I sit in the car for several minutes. I don't want to go home to my husband. Lucas is going to be so angry with me, and I'm not happy with him either. I think about my conversation with Natalie. What are the bonds that connect me and Lucas? I thought it was love, but I think my definition of love is warped. This relationship feels lately like it's based more on duty, fear, and control. I wouldn't say fear of Lucas, but fear of not being with him. I don't know what I would do if I was on my own. I fear that possibility, but I don't think I'm happy being with him either.

A movement toward the back of Natalie's townhouse catches my eye. I stare until I see it again. A person moves along the side of the house, stops, and seemingly stares directly at me sitting in the car. Tall, probably a man, but any features indistinguishable as the figure is cloaked in black, including a dark face mask. I keep my gaze on him, hoping to see something recognizable. His attention to me only last a few seconds, then he turns and disappears into the darkness of the trees and the rain pounds on top of my car, blurring any view of the interloper.

Who is that?

I stay parked in Natalie's driveway for another half hour or so. I don't want to drive in the heavy rains, I want to see if the person in black shows up again, and I don't want to go home to Lucas. The person I saw came from the rear of Natalie's house, perhaps from the backyard. I suppose it could be a neighbor, but why would a neighbor be sneaking around in a black face mask?

Could it be Lucas?

He knows Natalie and I are friends, and he hates it. Maybe he is looking for me since I'm not at home; he may have thought I'd be over here visiting her. But if it is him, he wouldn't have run off. He'd be in this car right now, probably yelling at me.

He's blowing up my phone with text and phone calls, none of which I answer. Now it is one thirty in the morning. I guess I have to go home at some point. Time to face the music.

. . .

Our pretty Cape Cod-style house is ablaze with light when I pull into the driveway and hit the garage door opener. As I pull into the garage, park the car, and close the door, Lucas opens the door from the kitchen.

His face is livid.

I glare at him and close the car door.

"Where were you?" he demands, blocking the doorway. "Why didn't you answer my calls?"

I brush past him and go into the kitchen. I walk to the cupboard, retrieve a glass, and get some water from the refrigerator dispenser. I take a long drink.

He slams the door and stands in the center of the kitchen watching me. I can see by his body language and the anger in his eyes, he's furious with me.

"Who were you with?" he growls. "Some guy?"

I look at him. "No, I wasn't with a guy. Why do you care? You went out without me."

He lets out a heavy sigh. "You didn't want to go. I asked you to come with me."

"You and your friends treat me like I'm dumb. You're always talking over me."

"I do not treat you that way!"

"It feels like it," I huff, putting the glass down.

"You still didn't answer me; where were you?"

"At Natalie's house," I say calmly.

He glares at me and gets in my face. "You're lying to me."

I back up. "No, I'm not." I meet his stare, his breath hot on my skin from his closeness, his anger radiating from his clenched fists and blazing eyes; I poke his chest, trying to push him away from me, waiting for his reaction—it could go either way.

"Don't push me away," he growls, moving even closer to me.

I don't back away this time. I meet his irate stare, our bodies almost touching, the anger between us seemingly like a third person in the room. Sweat trickles on my body.

"When did you get home?" I demand.

"Me! You're asking me when you're the one running around in the middle of the night with who knows who!" he yells.

"Yes, I am. When?"

"Like an hour ago!"

"Then why are you still wearing your coat?"

He stares at me like I'm crazy. He takes off his black coat and flings it on the kitchen table, and a piece of paper flies out the pocket onto the floor.

"I'm done talking to you. We'll talk when you can talk like an adult." He sighs. "I'm going to bed."

He stomps up the stairs and slams our bedroom door. I walk over to his coat and touch it, still slick with rain. If he was home an hour ago, wouldn't it be dry by now?

I bend down to retrieve the piece of trash. A green gum wrapper.

The same as the one on Natalie's porch.

TWENTY-SIX

Natalie

I staple the papers together and add the packet to the growing stack on my desk. I rearrange my inbox and sort the piles of paper on my desk, putting them in order. What a day. A virus is circulating around the school, unsurprisingly; at mid-October it's even a little later than normal. But it seems like everyone is getting sick, and once a few people get sick in a school, it spreads throughout the entire building. Anna threw up when she walked into my classroom, poor girl, and went home early. Olivia is out sick today too. I'm hoping Emma and I don't end up catching the bug.

My mind travels back to Saturday when Olivia called me to tell me about a man she saw standing outside my house on Friday night. The thought of it still gives me the creeps. She said the person was dressed in all black and wearing a face mask. Why would someone be prowling about, sneaking around our home? This must be the man Emma said she saw staring at our house, but why?

Something is going on. I've taken to closing all the curtains as soon as the light starts to fade, and triple-checking the lock every night before I go to bed.

Uneasiness travels through me thinking of someone lurking around watching me and Emma. Do they want to hurt me? Hurt us?

I don't know what to think at this point. Jake installed a Ring doorbell camera yesterday, so it somewhat soothes my nerves.

I worry about Olivia; our conversation was brief on Saturday, and I haven't spoken to her since then. She needs a friend more that I originally thought. There's something about having someone you can truly open up to about your feelings and fears that is such a relief. But I know that in order to take our friendship any further, I'd need to tell her about my own history with Lucas. It won't be today at least; she sent me a text last night saying she's sick and won't be in today. I'll text her tonight to check on her.

The last couple of days Lucas has been subdued. I've been rather enjoying it. But today is Wednesday and the old spark shows up when Haley and I walk into his classroom.

"Okay, class," he is saying, smiling at us. "Today we won't be doing math."

The students cheer.

"You're clearly very disappointed." He laughs. "But today we are joining Mrs. Dell's class for a guidance lesson with our wonderful guidance counselor, Mr. Miller."

Some students clap, others look bored. Some don't seem to care either way.

"Okay, let's line up. Remember to be quiet in the hall and"—he pauses—"I want you to be respectful of Mr. Miller."

The line of fourth graders nod. A few students in the back of the line are talking.

"I'll wait," Mr. Hanson says. "Until everyone is quiet."

A few minutes pass, then we travel two doors down the hall

to Mrs. Dell's classroom. We settle the students and I go to the back table to set my bag down. I rummage inside to retrieve a mint, but the box isn't in its normal pocket at the side of the bag; instead it's at the bottom buried under a pack of Post-it notes and a pack of tissues. I pop the wintergreen-flavored mint into my mouth.

The room is buzzing with chatter as Mr. Miller gets up to start his presentation. I look around for Lucas and Haley.

Both are gone.

Where did they go? I hurry up to Mrs. Dell.

"Excuse me, do you know where Lucas and Haley went?"

Debbie replies. "Probably the faculty room or his room. I told Lucas I'd stay the first half of the presentation and he can cover the second part. There's no point for both of us to be here the entire time. I guess Haley went with him."

"Oh, okay," I say. "I'll go check."

I hurry out the door and fly down to his classroom, flinging open the door.

Empty.

Crap. I head down the hall toward the faculty room. The playground must be muddy today because there are streaks of mud and grass all over the tile floor that I try to avoid. The gym is directly in front of me at the end of the hall; both entrance doors are closed, which is odd, usually both are open, but one is always open. I walk faster to reach my destination.

I peek into the rectangular window on the right door. Lucas and Haley are standing to the side of the gym talking closely, intimately. They are alone inside the space. Lucas then points to the stage area at the far end of the gym. The two begin to walk toward the stage.

Lucas has his hand on the small of her back.

Just like he did with Olivia at the carnival.

Just like he always did with me.

Creep.

I fling open the gym doors, and they loudly clang in the quiet hallway, as I intended them to do. They both turn, staring at me. Lucas's hand drops to his side. A nervous expression covers Haley's face.

"There you two are!" I say loudly. "I didn't know where you went. I was walking around looking for you two everywhere."

"Oh, yes," Lucas says, irritation in his voice. I enjoy making him angry. Really enjoy it. "Haley mentioned she hadn't been in the gym yet, so we decided to check it out on the way to the faculty room."

"Wonderful, nothing like a tour of an empty gym," I reply, sarcastically, a fake smile plastered on my face. "Looks like you were going to check out the stage. Shall we?"

"No, that's okay." Haley shrugs.

"Well, then." Lucas smiles. "I told Haley they filled the candy jar in the faculty room this morning. There might be peanut butter cups if we're lucky."

"Lead the way," I say.

"Oh, no." Lucas waves his hand. "After you."

I lead us out of the gym and down to the faculty room, burning with righteous anger.

Looks like Lucas can eat candy any damn time he pleases.

Unlike Olivia.

At the end of the day, Haley and I are in my classroom. Abby is still in Daphne's third-grade class for another ten minutes, so I decide it's a good time to talk to Haley.

I go to the back table and sit across from her. She's writing in her notebook and looks up at me. Her eyes widen.

"I wanted to talk a bit about this afternoon," I start. "It's not a good idea for you to go off alone with Mr. Hanson. He's married and much older than you." I clear my throat. I know I'm sounding ridiculous. "It's just not appropriate."

She considers me for a moment. "He was just showing me the gym."

"Why was his hand on your back?"

A blush heats her face.

"Haley, you know Mr. Hanson is married to Olivia," I say in a serious voice.

She sighs. "I know, but..."

I stare at her. "What?"

She lowers her voice. "She cheats on him. That's why he asked her to volunteer at school. So that he knows where she is when he's at work. Really, Mrs. A, we just talk to each other. I think Lucas just needs someone to talk about everything."

Anger fills me at his manipulative tactics. I hate this man *so* much! Who the hell does he think he is telling Haley personal things like this and things that are not even true! Olivia would never cheat on him. I take a deep breath. Great, so she's calling him Lucas now and he's telling her all kinds of made up "secrets."

"Haley, I'm sorry, but Lucas is lying to you. Olivia is not cheating on him. He is only telling you that to gain your trust. He should not be sharing things like that with you." I pause. "When did he tell you all of this? Are you texting with him?"

Haley shakes her head. She stands up and tosses her notebook into her bag. "Lucas said you would take her side. I'm sorry, I really like you, but I'm only being a friend to Mr. Hanson. I don't want to be rude, but you're kind of paranoid about all of this."

I sigh. "Please think about what I said. I'm not lying."

"Okay, I'm going now," and she is out the door.

When the hell did Lucas tell her all of these lies? I make sure I am always with her throughout the day. Then a thought occurs to me. I jump up and hurry out of my classroom, down to where the halls intersect. I see Haley walking down the fourth-grade hall. She stops at Lucas's room and goes inside.

She's been stopping in to see him before she leaves for the day. I'm always busy with bus duty at the other end of the school. This is when they are having all these heart-to-heart conversations. I am not going to allow him to wreak havoc on her life like he did to me. Heat fills me and my face burns with anger. He thinks he can do any damn thing he wants; he always has and he always gets away with it! Emotions wash over me and I take a few deep breaths to calm myself. But things are different now and I can put things in motion to change the outcome. I'm not a fifteen-year-old girl anymore. I can handle this and make the situation better for Haley and Olivia.

Sick or not, I must speak to Olivia tonight.

I have an IEP meeting after bus duty and after we finish the meeting I peek into Andrea Cameron's office, the building principal, but after the craziness of the afternoon I forgot that she's at a conference until next Tuesday.

I go back to my classroom and gather my things. Jake picked Emma up from school today since I have a meeting, and she will stay over at their house. He'll bring her to school tomorrow. I sit down at my desk and take a deep breath. I grab my phone and text Olivia.

> We have to talk.

Three dots.
They disappear. No message.
I try to call her, but it goes straight to voicemail.

> I'm sorry, Olivia, I know you aren't feeling well, but I need to talk to you.

I stare at my phone. Nothing.
I lay the phone on my desk. I walk to my whiteboard at the

front of the room, and I erase today's date and write tomorrow's date, then go back to my phone.

Olivia responded.

> I can't. I'm sorry Natalie.

What's going on with her? This can't be because she's sick. It must be because Lucas is telling her to stay away from me. I am so fed up with him. He makes me so angry the way he manipulates people.

Fuck you, Lucas!

Even though I only say those words in my mind, it makes me feel a bit better. A tried-and-true stress reliever.

I'm going to have to talk to Andrea about this situation with him. I'll keep it simple, tell her what I observed and that it appears inappropriate to me. Since nothing actually happened, Andrea will likely just talk to Lucas. That should cool things off between him and Haley, but he will know it was me who told Andrea, so how will he respond? Does he remember me yet? What if that was him lurking around my house on Friday night? I have to talk to Olivia first before I do anything.

When she came over to my house on Friday and we talked, I was tempted to tell her about my past with Lucas too. He'd preyed on both of us in the exact same way, taking advantage of his position and our trust to feed his desires.

Disgust fills me when I think about how he exploited my naivete and innocence. He wasn't only my first sexual partner, but my first kiss, my first everything. At the time, I was so in love with him, so eager to please him, so vigilant about keeping our relationship a secret and thinking hooking up in his office and a few gifts constituted a relationship. He even gave me a burner phone for our calls and texts so nobody would accidentally see them on my phone.

I wanted his touch, longed for it, hungered for his lips on

mine, his hands traveling down my body, pushing away the thin material of my shorts and underwear, slipping his fingers inside me as soon as practice was over and his office door was locked.

"Do you want this?" he'd ask.

"Yes," I'd whisper back.

I did want it.

But it shouldn't have been an option for me.

Not with him.

This realization took me years to understand. I went over it so many times in my mind back then. Did I want him too much? Was I obsessed with him? Yes and yes. Then after everything happened, I finally understood that none of that mattered.

I was a child, and he was an adult. None of it ever should have happened.

End of story.

TWENTY-SEVEN

Natalie

I crawl into bed, exhausted and hoping for a good night's sleep. I take off my glasses and place them on the nightstand. My head throbs, but I still look at my phone. I sent two more texts to Olivia tonight, both unanswered. Why is she pulling away from me now? Could Lucas be keeping her from me? He isn't exactly thrilled that the two of us are friends.

I pull the covers up to my chin and slowly drift into a fitful sleep. I don't know how long I slept, but at some point, familiar music lures me from my slumber. Classical music filters into my mind. At first, I thought it was from memory but then I sit up in bed. It's not in my memory.

Where is it coming from?

I listen intently and then stumble out of bed. I stand in the center of my room. The music is loud, but not overpowering, a creepy background score to an otherwise quiet night.

I walk over to my bedroom window and the music is louder. I lift the window and the screen beneath, the cool night air piercing through my thin nightgown. I peer down into the backyard, and I don't see anything unusual, but the classical melody continues to play. Goosebumps prick my neck and my arms tingle as I stretch my body to gain a better look. Moonlight illuminates the backyard: Emma's dark green swing set with an attached playhouse; a small gardening shed to the right of it; a patio table with four chairs surrounding it; and a sand box at the rear of the yard filled with various toys. I squint harder, but while the volume of the music seems to rise, I still cannot see anything unusual.

Should I go out and look around? Maybe the neighbor is playing music, but that would be odd behavior at this time of night for the older couple that lives next door. The husband works night shift and his wife, Brenda, is a night owl, but is usually downstairs in their recently remodeled basement watching movies. I scan the area again from my lookout point, then go downstairs.

Is the music being used as a lure to bait me outside? Or am I being paranoid?

I put on my slippers and robe and hurry downstairs to the sliding glass doors that open to the small patio and backyard. I stare out the glass doors, then pluck a flashlight from the kitchen drawer. The only way someone would have access to our backyard, other than this door, is to climb over the eight-foot fence. The yard is empty now, except for what is supposed to be there, and the music which seems to increase in volume.

I slide the door open—it squeaks loudly halfway through—and I step onto the patio. The music blares as I step onto the concrete patio and then onto the grass. I glance at the patio table, chairs, and the lounge chair to the left, nothing out of order. I make my way to the swing set, taking in the swings, slide, and small climbing wall that makes up the outdoor structure. I climb up the wooden stairs and peek into the playhouse.

Empty. Then I walk toward the small garden shed. I put my hand on the door and pull it open.

The music stops.

I start and whirl around, searching the yard for something unusual.

Or someone.

The backyard is silent now. Silvery moonlight flooding the small space, creating shadows and eerie movement in the night. I stand for several minutes, watching and listening for any movement, any sound, but none comes. I turn back to the shed and pull open the door, shining my flashlight to survey its contents. A half-empty bag of mulch, gardening tools, some of Emma's outdoor toys, and a few extra resin chairs.

The music has concluded its melody, but I'm certain it was intended for an audience of one.

Me.

I shiver in the cool evening air and run back into the house, locking the patio door behind me. Why is this happening to me? I close the blinds on the patio door and sink to the floor, tears spilling from my eyes. Why can't I just have a quiet life? That's all I want. Who is doing all of these strange things around our house? What do they want?

I turn around and face the closed blinds, taking my finger and raising one slat, peering out into the dark backyard. The moon shines above and for a moment I think I see a movement inside Emma's playhouse on her swing set. A flash of light and a shadowy figure.

Who, or what is it?

Panic snakes through me and I drop the slat. Slowly, I open it again and stare outside. I stare for a long time. No movement or light this time.

I wasn't alone in that backyard.

. . .

I don't sleep well the rest of the night and when the alarm goes off its piercing ring only adds to my massive headache. I pull myself out of the bed; my body aches and I'm sweating. I'm sick.

I grab my laptop from the nightstand and email Mindy, the school secretary, to tell her I will be out today and attach my emergency sub plans. I give instructions that the substitute needs to stay with Haley the entire time she is there. I hope a teacher sub is available; the school is desperately low on substitutes this year.

Mindy emails me a short time later. She says the building sub is available to cover me, and I breathe a sigh of relief. I text Jake too. He replies that Candace will pick Emma up from school today and he hopes I feel better.

I fall back into bed, my head pounding, praying for sleep to envelop me in its warm embrace, but it doesn't arrive. I pull myself out of bed again and trudge to the bathroom, fumbling around in the medicine cabinet for the cold medicine. I swallow the two pills and fill my paper cup again; the cold water is welcome relief for my parched mouth. My thoughts drift to the weird music from last night. Should I report it to the police? I doubt they would do anything about something like that. Really, what am I going to say, I heard classical music playing in the middle of the night and then I didn't? I will ask Jake to install another Ring camera, this time at the back door. And now, I'm too sick to even speculate about it.

TWENTY-EIGHT

Him

She never notices the speaker I hid on her daughter's slide in the backyard the other night. Come on, Natalie, you're supposed to be so smart; where else would music be coming from but a speaker? Although, admittedly it was quite small and well-hidden if I do say so myself.

I move to the side yard and slither under the loose boards at the back, loosened by me, and carefully move toward the backdoor, now securely locked, but I made a copy of the key I found under the planter days ago. I might as well use it now. I'm sure she'll have that ex-husband install another camera at the back door as he did on the front.

The house is silent as I expected at ten in the morning on a school day, and I stand in her kitchen listening and move a few things around just for fun. A sponge from the sink is put on the kitchen table. A stack of books is moved from the table to the floor. I pick up one of her daughter's dolls from the living room and sit it on the stairs. Silly things really, but it makes me laugh.

I like to laugh.

I walk through the living room and ascend the stairs, quietly and carefully as always. I pause at the daughter's bedroom, but she's not there; sometimes I visit at night while the little girl sleeps soundly, covered in a unicorn comforter, her curly dark hair splayed on the crisp white pillowcase. Innocent and darling, as always.

I move on to her mother's room. A neat, tidy room not necessarily stylish, but comfortable with a gray and white geometric print comforter that she slides under at night to sleep. I've been in this room while Natalie sleeps too, on some occasions, just watching her, different thoughts in my mind for her. But that's not why I'm here. I spy her pink bathrobe carelessly tossed on the chair by the bed.

I take the robe and tiptoe out of the room.

TWENTY-NINE

Natalie

I feel like myself the next day and go into school early to read the sub's notes and catch up on what I missed. I'm sitting at my desk when Andrea, the principal, walks in. I sigh, about to tell her what I witnessed on Wednesday. The matter can't be delayed any longer, even if I haven't spoken to Olivia. I'm still feeling queasy about the strange music playing in my yard the other night and the movement I saw in the playhouse. I inspected everything in the light of day, but found nothing unusual. What the hell was that about? I have to figure out what's going on at home. But first, Andrea.

"Natalie," Andrea says. She's dressed in a smart-looking periwinkle blouse and black dress pants. "May I talk to you for a moment?"

"Sure, I want to talk to you too," I reply. My palms sweat and I wipe them on my dress pants. Why does she want to talk to *me*?

She pulls a chair up across from my desk. "Lucas spoke to

me yesterday. I guess there was some misunderstanding between you two about Haley," she begins.

I stare at her. Of course he approached her first; I should have guessed he would. "Yes, not a misunderstanding, but Lucas is too friendly with Haley and sharing personal information with her."

Andrea nods. "Yes, he told me. I also spoke to Haley, but she assures me there is nothing inappropriate between them."

I begin to fluster. "But he told her his wife was cheating on him. He shouldn't be sharing things like that with her."

"She mentioned you have been overly concerned with Lucas and Olivia's marriage, and Lucas has the same concerns," she says seriously. "I also spoke to Olivia yesterday."

My eyes widen.

"Okay, what did she say?" What kind of set up is this? I'm overly concerned about Lucas and Olivia's marriage? I'm being set up as the problem, not Lucas. He's the problem!

"She said she didn't want to volunteer in your room anymore. She has some other things which need her focus."

"What?"

"You're new to the school, Natalie; I think all of this was a misunderstanding and nobody holds ill feelings. The best thing is just to move on."

I'm quiet, unsure of what to do. Lucas has painted a pretty picture for Andrea bringing Haley and Olivia along with him. If I keep insisting, I'm going to be the one who is pushed out. He's trying to say I'm obsessed with him. Why am I not surprised about this turn of events? I should have seen it coming.

"Oh, okay," I say. "Yes, let's move on."

"Thank you, Natalie." Andrea stands. "I'm glad you're feeling better."

"Thank you." I force a smile as she walks out of the room.

I take a sip of my coffee that I picked up in the faculty room, regretting not being able to be the one to speak to Andrea first. Although I'm not sure if it would have mattered. It seems as if Lucas and Andrea are close, and I'm the outsider. I want to do the right thing here, but I feel completely alone. If I continue to push by myself, Lucas will find a way to crush me. I need Olivia on my side.

Haley and I enter Lucas's classroom. She and I spoke earlier, her insisting I misunderstood what she told me about Olivia and that Lucas was simply showing her the gym. I pushed her with more questions, but she stuck to her story, obviously coached by Lucas. He must have a closer hold on her than I originally thought. Which worries me—just how deep is she in his clutches? I end our conversation by telling her she can come to me anytime to talk about anything. I hope she will.

Lucas has two math problems up on the SMART Board and is discussing them with the class. Haley stands on one side of the room by Heather and I'm on the other side, by Dylan and Sam. I stare at Lucas, seemingly innocuous, in his red button down and gray pants, friendly face and engaging manner. All I can think of is how he turned my life down such a heartbreaking avenue and the years I suffered because of it. And Olivia, scared to eat a cookie, because he wouldn't like it and how he made her quit volunteering; I'm sure it wasn't because it's what she wanted. Finally, Haley, willing to cover and lie for him. Little does she know this is only the beginning for her.

This power he wields is so influential and consuming, good looks, a practiced gregarious personality, and a pattern of conditioning that works perfectly on young women entering womanhood, new at romantic relationships. If he was unattractive and quiet, he wouldn't be half as dangerous.

Predator is the only word for him. I'm getting so angry just looking at him. I take a deep breath; I can't allow emotions to rule me, I must stay calm.

"Okay, class," Lucas is saying. "I'm going to hand out a worksheet with five problems. Try them and we will go over them as a class. These are not going to be graded; I just feel we need more practice on these."

He goes to his desk, grabs a stack of papers, and hands them to Haley.

"Will you hand these out?" he asks, smiling at her.

"Sure." She returns the smile and accepts the papers.

He looks at me. "May I speak with you for a moment in the hall?"

"Sure," I say, walking toward the door with him following.

We stand outside his door.

"Did Andrea speak to you this morning?" he asks.

"She did."

"I wanted to make everything clear with no misinterpretation for anyone. Andrea and I are good friends and I felt strongly that I needed to include her," he says, his gaze intent on me. He moves close to me. Too close.

"You certainly did that," I counter, my agitation with him growing as I stare at him. This is the closest proximity I've been to him since I started working here. He's trying to intimidate me, and part of me wants to give in, to back away, but I stand my ground. I will not allow him to intimidate me. "I am very clear."

A flit of confusion crosses his face. Or is it recognition? Apprehension runs through me. The last thing I need is for him to recognize me.

"And Olivia won't be coming in anymore?" I ask. We are so close that his shirt sleeve is almost touching mine. "How does she feel about that?"

A ripple of anger is evident in his narrowing eyes, then

dissolves. "Oh, she'll still volunteer for special events." He lowers his voice to a whisper. "Like *I* want her to, *Natalie*."

"Good for you." I open the classroom door and walk inside, leaving him staring at me from the hallway. Relief spreads through me as I retreat from our too close contact.

What am I going to do about him?

THIRTY

Natalie

Saturday night at the hibachi restaurant always proves to be a busy, fun environment. We sit around the grill and the chef grills chicken and chops vegetables. He points to Ryan and tosses a piece of chicken to him, which he catches in his mouth.

"Nice catch!" I exclaim, laughing.

"Thanks." He grins, chewing the chicken.

The chef makes his onion volcano, and everyone oohs and claps as it flames, and a few minutes later our food is sizzling on our plates.

"I love hibachi places," I remark, popping some broccoli into my mouth. "It's so fun."

"I agree," says Ryan. "I worked at a place like this in college, but I was a host and a waiter, not a cool chef."

I laugh again. "I worked in a restaurant in college too. I was a waitress."

"How did you like it?"

"It was okay; tips were pretty good."

Ryan smiles, his hazel eyes sparking. I had forgotten how

much I enjoy talking to him. He looks good tonight in a dark green pullover that highlights the green flecks in his eyes and his mop of thick, dark curly hair.

"That means a lot in college," he replies, spearing another piece of chicken.

"Sure does. How's your new puppy?" I ask. "What's his name?"

"Tucker," he replies. "But I usually call him Tuck."

"That's a great name."

"I think so; he's a handful though, always chewing my socks."

"I bet Emma would love him."

He looks at me. "You should bring her over sometime to meet Tuck."

I smile at him. "Maybe I will."

"How are things going at your new job?"

I fiddle with my napkin. "It's okay."

He looks at me again. "Some issues?"

"Some, but nothing I can't handle."

"I have no doubt of that," he states. "Anything I can help with?"

I shake my head. "No, but I appreciate you asking."

Ryan meets my gaze. "Of course, anything you need, anytime, just call me."

I smile and focus on my food. I feel a blush flooding my face.

I brush my teeth absentmindedly while my mind replays my evening with Ryan. I forgot how much I enjoy talking to him. It was so easy to have a conversation with him and I love his intelligence and humor. We worked together for four years; he started at my old school after I'd worked there about a year. For second grade, most of the students on my caseload were usually assigned to his classroom because he had the understanding and patience that students with special needs require. I would then either push in for whole group instruction, while supporting my students, or pull my students out for small group instruction for core subjects. I had a large group of second graders my last year at the school, so Ryan and I spent much of that school year together. We made a good team and became good friends. For a second, I toy with the idea of reconsidering my friends-only policy. Thoughts of Ryan's smile and the way he makes me feel fill my mind. Maybe someday.

A quick rinse of my mouth and I go into the bedroom to retrieve my robe, but it isn't lying across the chair where I usually put it. Odd, I walk back into the bathroom to see if I hung it on the hook at the back of the door. Nope.

Did I leave it downstairs? I hurry downstairs and check the living room, kitchen, and the bathroom. No robe. This is strange. I travel back up the stairs and look through my bedroom again. I rifle through the closet, look under the bed even though I have no idea how it would have gotten under there. Nothing but a few dust bunnies. Okay, more than a few.

I get up and go over to Emma's room and check all the possible areas, but no luck.

Where in the world is my robe?

Could Emma have put it somewhere? I go back to my room and text Jake.

> Hey, will you ask Emma if she put my robe somewhere?

> OK.

A few minutes pass until a text pops up.

> No, she said she didn't.

> OK, thanks.

> How was your date? 😊

>> Ha! It wasn't a date.

> Well...???

I smile at the phone.

>> I had a great time. Ryan is a great guy.

> Good. I'm glad.

>> Thanks, I'm glad too.

I lay my phone down. I have no clue where my robe could be. I don't remember putting it in the wash. I grab a sweatshirt instead and go into the bathroom to sort through the hamper, nothing. Then I go downstairs to search the laundry down there by the washer, nothing again. This is getting ridiculous. A robe doesn't just disappear.

Could someone have taken it?

Thoughts of the Barbie doll assault me, and the strange music from the other night. But if someone took my robe...

They would have been inside my house.

I shiver, not wanting to think about it. I grab my phone and look at the Ring camera footage from the last few days. An Amazon delivery driver, the mailman, Jake, nothing unusual, but this only shows the front door. Jake is going to install another camera at the back door tomorrow when he brings Emma home.

Even though I don't think Lucas recognizes me, I know he doesn't like me. He detests my friendship with Olivia. But this stuff seems too creepy for him. Although, I knew him twenty years ago; so much can change in that many years. My deepest fear is that Theo is out of prison. But then, all of this seems too subtle for him. I know nothing. Only that I'm scared, and I want it to stop.

I'm not going to waste any more time searching for the robe. I go into the kitchen, get a bottle of water and head back upstairs. I check my closet, under my bed and in every nook and cranny someone could hide, but thankfully everything is empty. Then I lock my bedroom door. This is getting ridiculous, locking myself inside my bedroom in my own house, but I still think of that movement in the yard, the music, and all the other odd occurrences happening here. *Someone* is doing this. I'm going to have to start sleeping in Emma's bed with her when she's here, and I'll lock her bedroom door too. I shake my head.

That's no way to live.

I get into bed and flick on the TV, settling on a romantic comedy. Something light is what I need. I look at my phone lying on the nightstand, tempted to text Olivia again. I sent another yesterday after that uncomfortable discussion with Lucas in the hall, but she still hasn't responded. I wish I knew what is going on with her. I'm worried.

Olivia is my key to revealing Lucas's true nature. He has everyone else wrapped around his finger with his manipulations. Olivia and I are the only ones who see beyond the handsome mask and the flirty sweet talk. I thought Olivia might even be ready to pull away from Lucas after her revelation to me about Haley's notebook and the issues she and Lucas have been having, but now she doesn't even return my texts.

Did something happen to her? I don't have any reasonable explanation of why she'd be avoiding me. I take a sip of water mulling over everything. Something is wrong. I know she would answer my calls and texts—none of this makes any sense to me. She told me where they live, so maybe I'll drop by her house and check on her.

What did Lucas do to keep her silent?

THIRTY-ONE

Olivia

I pick up my phone and flick through Natalie's numerous texts that I haven't answered. I take a sip of the protein shake Lucas made for me before he left to go golfing. It's a Monday and normally he'd have school, but was off for Columbus Day. He's really been into protein shakes lately and insists I drink one every morning. I want to answer Natalie's texts, but so much more is at stake now, and I want to make sure I, we, move in the right direction. I don't know what to tell her; things are different now, I have so much to consider. And I still have so many unanswered questions. I place my shake back on the table and rub my stomach. So much more to consider.

I need answers.

I agreed with Lucas's demand that I stop volunteering in Natalie's room; it is easier to do so than continue to argue, and he always wins anyway. He didn't let up until he did, as usual.

Another text pops up from Natalie.

> I'm coming over to your house.

>> OK

I type.

Natalie must have heard that Lucas is playing golf today—if that is what he's doing—she wouldn't stop by if he's home, I'm sure. He's been sneering about her all week. He seems to think she has a problem with him and is keeping an eye on his actions.

She's not the only one.

I rise from the sofa, with laptop in hand, and walk to the kitchen. I place it on the kitchen table and then put on a pot of coffee. I'll need strong coffee for this meeting. I harbor strong concerns about Lucas and it's funny that she seems to understand them, which surprises and comforts me. I finally feel like I have an ally. I walk upstairs to our ensuite bathroom and stare at the pregnancy test sitting on the vanity counter, not too far from a brand-new box of tissues I placed there yesterday. I can't look away as my emotions struggle to determine my feelings about it.

A sharp knock raps on my front door, and I hurry down the stairs to answer it. I open the door and Natalie stands there, dressed in jeans and a dark pink sweater that looks good with her dark hair and eyes. She appears hesitant but determined.

"Thank God, Olivia," she says. "I've been worried about you."

"I'm okay, I just needed some time. Come in."

"Lucas is golfing today, right? I overheard him talking in the faculty room."

I nod. "He is. He won't be home for hours."

She nods and walks inside.

"Would you like some coffee?" I ask.

She nods again and I pour the coffee into two mugs. "Cream?"

"Yes, please."

We sit across from each other at the kitchen table. Natalie is studying me.

"I'm glad you're doing well," she says, taking a sip of coffee. "I was worried about you."

I sigh. "I know, I'm sorry; so much has happened this week."

"With you and Lucas?"

"Yes, with him."

"Why did you tell Andrea you wanted to stop volunteering in my classroom? You're not upset with me, are you?"

"No, of course not," I assure her, meeting her gaze. "No problems with you. It's Lucas."

She nods. "I figured as much but wanted to check. I want to tell you what happened on Wednesday. I'm sure Lucas told you his version, but here's what happened." She proceeds to tell me the details.

Anger surges within me as she continues, right down to Haley telling Natalie that Lucas said I was cheating on him.

"He said I was cheating? He told Haley that?" I jump up and pace around the kitchen. "The liar!"

Tears sting my eyes, but I will not allow them to fall. I will not let him do that to me again. Why I have allowed him to rule my life for so many years I'll never know.

"I guess he didn't mention that part of the story to you," Natalie replies.

"Funny how he failed to mention that detail," I laugh ruefully. "He pleaded with me to stop volunteering in your room and had me call Andrea to confirm. I guess I was another little piece of his puzzle, like always."

"Not surprising. I think your suspicions about Haley and him are correct and they may be more involved than we thought."

I have to get answers. Thinking about him cheating on me is tearing me up inside.

He's probably with her right now.

A sick feeling comes over me and I jump up to run to the

bathroom, throwing up in the toilet. I splash water on my face and rinse my mouth, trying to calm myself. I walk out of the bathroom. My eyes meet Natalie's.

"I have an idea," I say to her. "Let's follow him and see what he's really doing when he says he's golfing every Saturday. Will you help me?"

She pauses, hesitant. A few moments pass. "I don't really like this idea, but I think you need answers. Yes, I'll help you."

My stomach churns again. I'm going to find the truth whether I like it or not.

THIRTY-TWO

Natalie

Saturday morning rolls around and Olivia and I crouch in my car outside the restaurant where Lucas has met Haley for lunch. They sit on the shady patio, dining on club sandwiches and soup while I keep snapping photos with the expensive camera I borrowed from Jake last night.

My car is parked at the far end of the parking lot, beside a large pickup truck on one side and a dumpster on the other side, so we are mostly hidden while doing our undercover work. I continue to snap pictures, and Olivia sits beside me. She hasn't said a word since we arrived.

It's ridiculous, really, but she insisted we follow him to get some answers. I parked my car on a side street by Olivia's house, and she jumped in a minute or two after Lucas left for the supposed golf course. Luckily, he drove fairly slow so I didn't have any trouble catching up with him, following at a reasonable distance to avoid exposure. Being here now, my heart racing, my senses alert, it's rather exciting for me, but certainly devastating for her. I continue to zoom and snap with Jake's camera and hope some of the shots are decent. It's pretty amazing how up close and personal the photos are on the screen when using the zoom.

"I can't do this." Olivia's voice wavers. "I can't watch him out on a date. What's he thinking?"

I lower the camera and look at her. "I'm sorry, this must be hard for you. You wanted to do this, remember, you said you needed to know."

She nods. "I needed to see it myself."

I shake my head. "I didn't think this was a good idea, but I think it's better if you know though. And we were right, he is seeing Haley. If you want to go now, we can."

"No," she snaps, her eyes narrow. "I should go in there right now and confront him."

"No, don't do it, you're not ready to confront him," I say quickly. "You're just going to make a scene and he'll talk his way out of it. You know that."

She's quiet, but just continues to stare at them enjoying their intimate lunch.

I snap three more pictures. "Are you okay?"

She shakes her head. "How can I be okay? He's my husband. I don't hate him like you do."

I look at her. "Why would you say that?"

"I saw the way you looked at him the other day in the office," she says, tears in her eyes. "Did he come on to you too? Is this what he does, tries to have sex with everyone?" she screams.

"No, shhh..." I say, looking around, but nobody is within earshot—we're parked far enough away. "He-he's not trying to have sex with me."

"Why did I believe him?"

I don't say anything, and we sit in silence. Olivia is silent, but her hands are twitching, and her eyes are closed. She's breathing heavily. I never should have agreed to do this with her, but she practically begged me.

Finally, they stand up to leave.

"They're leaving, wake up, Olivia," I say, nudging her gently.

Her eyes fly open. "I'm awake. Do you think I'm going to fall asleep on a stakeout?"

I laugh. I can't control myself. "A stakeout?"

She looks at me and nervous laughter explodes from her. "This is so crazy!"

We watch them exit the restaurant and enter Lucas's SUV, leaving Haley's car in the restaurant parking lot. We follow at a reasonable distance to a park not too far from the restaurant.

"I know you don't want to see it," I say to Olivia. "But if we can get a picture or two of them touching or kissing, we'll have proof to take to Andrea. He won't be able to talk his way out of it."

"I guess," Olivia says, her eyes sad.

Luckily, it's a beautiful day and the parking lot is full. They park toward the front entrance, and we take a spot toward the end. They exit the vehicle and walk along the paved trail into the park.

We scramble out of my car and, camera in hand, walk a good distance behind them but keeping them loosely in view. As soon as we can, we move into the substantial wooded area surrounding the pathways.

Lucas and Haley walk slowly along the path, not touching, but deep in conversation, close, intimate. We crouch behind clumps of trees, and I snap pictures while Olivia grimaces and wrings her hands.

"I've seen enough," she whispers to me. "Let's go."

I pause, conflicted. I don't want to go; we haven't gotten any real evidence, just a few photos of them eating lunch together. If I'm going to show these to the principal I need something substantial, them kissing or something physical. I look over to Olivia, who is wringing her hands again. Her face is pale and drawn, her eyes downcast. I push my feelings aside; this is too much for her.

We hurry out of the park and into the car.

"I'm never doing this again," Olivia says in a voice barely above a whisper. "I can't."

THIRTY-THREE

Natalie

On Sunday afternoon, I rummage through the kitchen cabinets, jotting down items we need at the grocery store. I glance at the clock. I'd have enough time to dash there and be home before Jake drops Emma at home, but I'd better wait. She likes to pick her own snacks for school at the store. She also likes to push the small grocery cart that the store has for children around the store, putting in her selections.

A quick survey of the refrigerator has me adding milk, eggs, and yogurt to the list. I close the door and listen to the quiet house, then peek into the adjoining living room, eyeing my pink bathrobe lying over the sofa. I found my robe this morning, mostly lying behind the sofa, only one arm dangling over the top. It seems impossible that I could have missed it when searching for it, but how else did it get there? Also, improbable that someone took it and then hid it behind the sofa. What would be the point?

Regardless, the locksmith will be here tomorrow after school to change the locks. With all the unusual happenings around here that's the least I can do to be proactive and make sure Emma and I are safe. And when that is finished, I still have other fish to fry.

Like Lucas.

Olivia surprised me by wanting to follow Lucas, although once on the scene I wasn't surprised how she clammed up. She was right about him and even though she said she's not following him again, I'm not taking that same stance. Olivia gave me the idea, but I'm going to see it through, and get the evidence we need to take him down. I know it's not easy for her to stand up for herself. I hope that she makes more decisions that are based on what she wants or needs versus what Lucas thinks she should. It's the only way she's going to build confidence in herself.

We have a plan to go to Haley's house on Tuesday after school. I told Jake I have a meeting, so he'll pick Emma up from school. On Tuesdays and Thursdays Haley has cheerleading practice at the high school until six p.m., so it's the perfect time to speak to her parents, hopefully at least one of them. I contacted Hannah, the high school guidance counselor, for her address and phone number, telling her I'd like to reach out to her parents, perhaps to send a card or call, to express what a wonderful job Haley is doing through the work study program in my class. I'll try to call first, but we're stopping by regardless. I'm hoping after speaking to her parents I can go to Andrea with them and with the photos we took on Saturday. Although I don't know how all the logistics will work out.

I glance at the robe again. I have more than one dilemma to figure out. It still bothers me how this robe disappeared and showed up again. There must be an explanation for it. I'm tired of strange things happening around here; I only want a quiet life, but I've anything but that.

. . .

I cover Emma with a blanket and turn down the volume on the TV. She fell asleep about forty-five minutes into the movie. It had been a busy evening with her dance class after school and running errands. I should get her ready for bed, but I'll let her sleep a bit. I stare at her angelic face and softly smooth back her hair. How did I get so lucky to have such a sweet child? She's the gift I never deserved but I treasure more than my own life. I hope that I can always protect her from the evils of life.

I sit for a few more minutes admiring her, then remember in the busyness of the evening I never picked up my mail today. I get up and walk out the front door, down our short driveway to the mailbox, and retrieve the short stack of mail inside.

I take it inside and sit at the kitchen table to sort through it. Some junk mail, a credit card bill and what looks like a card in a pale blue envelope with a typed label addressed to me. Odd, it isn't my birthday or any other holiday that would warrant a card. I tear it open and pull out a white card decorated with red and pink hearts. I frown and open it. The card is blank, but a typed poem is pasted inside.

Roses are Red
Violets are Blue
Hearts are Forever
I'm Thinking of You

A shiver races up my spine as I reread the card. Under the poem is a handwritten question mark.

Who sent this to me?

I study the card, front, inside, and back, plus the envelope.

Ryan?

The roses he left were a sweet thought, after I understood the joke on the card, but this is... creepy.

We have been having a great time together lately, but we are still only friends; we haven't crossed that line. Is his interest in me more intense than I realize?

My nerves rattle inside me all day on Tuesday. Everything distracts me and I jump at the slightest disturbance. I can't stop thinking about what we're going to do after school.

"Natalie." Abby walks over to me, looking at me in a motherly fashion. "Are you okay?"

I nod. "Yeah, maybe coming down with a cold."

She looks at me warily. "You just don't seem like yourself today. Can I do anything to help you?"

She is very kind, and I appreciate her concern. "Well, could you stay in the room for a few minutes? I need to go to the bathroom, but my reading intervention group will soon be here."

"Sure, no problem." Abby smiles.

"They can read over the vocab words until I get back," I say, sailing out of the door.

"Sounds good," she replies.

I hurry down to the faculty room to the private bathroom in the back of the room. I don't have to use the bathroom but need to calm my frayed nerves. I slept terribly last night. All this business with Haley and Lucas is dredging up memories I thought I long since buried. I don't have time to think about old sorrows; I have Emma to concentrate on now. I didn't want to feel those old painful regrets again. I felt them for so many years. There's a new feeling of guilt though: that I haven't told Olivia about my past. I want to tell her, but I feel she's so fragile now with what's happening with Haley and Lucas. He manipulated Olivia into a false portrayal of himself, and she fully believed it for many years and only now is realizing he's very different. I don't want to hurt her further, but I realize if I continue to keep the information from her it will hurt her more.

My reflection stares back at me in the mirror over the bathroom sink. It's funny how the body ages but the feelings inside never do. No, you don't remember everything, but you remember how situations or actions made you feel. Lost, hopeless, in pain, with no voice in things that have a direct impact on you. No choice! I hate thinking about that period of my life. My heart and mind told me the right choice to make, but circumstances prohibited me and now I can never go back and change it.

No matter how much I want to do so.

I take a deep breath and try to recenter myself. I must put away my own personal feelings and focus on the task at hand. This visit is about Haley and her decisions and future. I have an important job this afternoon when Olivia and I speak to Haley's parents. I haven't had any luck reaching them by phone, but I'm hoping someone will be at the house when we stop by later today.

I need to protect Haley. I want her to have choices.

Like I didn't.

THIRTY-FOUR

Natalie

Haley lives in the trailer park on the outskirts of town.

When we enter the park, most of the mobile homes appear newer and well-kept, but as we move deeper into the park, the upkeep seems to go downhill. Flowerpots with brightly colored flowers and welcoming front porches with comfortable-looking rocking chairs are replaced with sagging front porches, weed-filled flower beds and broken-down cars surrounded by high grasses. A few children walk along the stone road—a couple I recognize from school—after the school bus drops them off at the front of the park. We drive along the stone road that travels through the park, reading the numbers listed on the homes until we locate Haley's. Olivia drives; she told Lucas she has a doctor's appointment, and she picked me up. Now we travel in her black SUV in search of Haley's parents.

We're almost at the end of the park when we find Haley's home. A decrepit white trailer with faded blue trim. A ramshackle enclosed porch sits at the entrance, holes missing from its screening; the door swings open and shut, squeaking in the breeze of the afternoon. High weeds encircle the structure, with a few random wildflowers poking through. An old Ford Escort is parked outside, obviously having seen better days. This can't be where Haley lives.

"Is this right?" I look at the address again. "Yes, it is. I don't picture Haley living here."

"Let's get this over with." Olivia pulls in next to the Ford Escort and parks. She's tight with tension as she grabs her folder containing the photos from the backseat.

"Yes, let's go."

We exit the vehicle and enter through the open screened porch door. Trash fills the dark space, and we kick various fast-food wrappers out of our way as we walk to the front door. A few lawn chairs sit to the right side, one stacked up with magazines. A white planter filled with dead leaves sits next to them.

Olivia and I look at each other, then I ring the doorbell, but no sound emits, so I knock on the door. I'm still having a hard time believing that this is Haley's house. She's so neat and well dressed, but maybe I'm making assumptions; perhaps the inside of the house is different, and her parents may be very nice. I must keep an open mind and not draw conclusions from what I'm seeing on the surface. There's a scuffling inside, but nobody appears at the door. I knock again, harder this time. More scuffling. Somebody is inside, but I'm not sure if they will answer the door.

The door creaks open. A thin woman with scraggly blonde hair stands in front of us. She wears cut-off jean shorts and a worn white sweatshirt with a huge brown stain on the front. She smiles at us, her teeth yellow with plaque. Her left front tooth is chipped. Her eyes appear tired and a bit glassy.

"Yous from the church?" she asks. "I'll take that free food again. I liked that soup you brought last time."

I shake my head. "No, we're from the school. We wanted to talk about Haley. Is she your daughter?"

"Oh." The woman is visibly disappointed. "Yeah, she's one of them. I got three daughters. Haley's the last one at home. All the rest got themselves boyfriends and moved out of here. Lucky them."

"May we come in?" I ask. "I'm Natalie Amaryllis, Haley is working in my room in the afternoons for her work placement, and this is Olivia."

"Oh, yeah. Haley's got some idea about being a teacher. Don't know how she thinks she's gonna do that, all that fancy book learnin'." The woman laughs, a rough guttural laugh. Spittle flies onto my shirt—due to our close distance—and I cringe. "We're not college money people." She motions us to come inside.

"Well, there's lots of ways to go to college," I say. "Grants, loans, Haley is a smart girl. I'm sure if she is determined she will find a way to do it."

"Too damn smart for her britches sometimes, that girl," the woman says. "Too many big ideas. It's better if you know where you come from and be done with it. Too much dreaming makes you disappointed."

I think this may be the first time I heard a parent complain that their child is too smart. Usually, parents are very happy if their child has dreams, aspirations, and intelligence. Seeing where Haley lives and meeting her mother makes me admire all her accomplishments. And determined that she won't waste them.

We stand in the middle of the living room. A long brown sofa sits across from us, piled with various clothing, a coffee table in front of it littered with beer cans and dirty dishes. The TV is on but turned down very low. The floor is littered with more clothes, paper trash, and more empty beer cans. I'm not sure where to go. I spy a small table in the kitchen that looks semi clean.

"Can we sit at the table?" I ask. "What is your name?"

"Lydy," she answers. "Sure, let's sit."

The table only has a few takeout flyers on it and there are four clean chairs to sit on, thankfully. We settle in and I smile at Haley's mother. Olivia looks very tense and uncomfortable sitting across from me. I'm not sure what's going on with her, then I remember we are talking about her husband: Despite the troubles they have, this still must be incredibly hurtful for her.

"Lydy," I start. "I have a bit of a concern about Haley. We have some information that she may be spending time out of school with a male teacher."

"Oh." Lydy seems unconcerned. She goes to the refrigerator and retrieves a beer. "You two want one?"

Olivia and I shake our heads, refusing the offer.

"Here." Olivia pulls out the photos. Her hands shake.

Lydy stares at them. "Yeah, looks like they are on a date. That guy is good-looking. Good for her. Haley knows how to pick 'em. That's a lot nicer date than I've ever gone on. Usually, it's just a six pack on the back of a pickup truck."

"Haley is sixteen and this is a teacher she works with. It's not appropriate," I say, in a stern tone. "I want to make you aware so you can talk to Haley about it, about making good choices, smart choices. And I thought perhaps you would like to speak to the principal at the school with us about the situation."

Lydy stares at me like I'm insane. She shoves the pictures back at Olivia. "What are you talking about? So, Haley got herself a new boyfriend, good for her. Why do you care? You say he's a teacher. Good, maybe he can pay for her college. I'm sure as hell not. Maybe he'll be her ticket out of this place." She laughs. "Maybe I should date him; I bet he has a nice house."

"Lydy!" a deep male voice yells from the bedroom. An overweight man walks out into the kitchen wearing only boxer shorts. "Where's my beer?"

He stops and looks at us. "Who are these people?"

"I dunno. They're worried because Haley has a boyfriend."

Lydy laughs again. "She's sixteen. That girl ain't no nun. What sixteen-year-old girl doesn't have a boyfriend?"

"Haley?" The man sounds confused, like he's just woken up from a nap.

"My daughter, you idiot."

"Oh, yeah."

Lydy throws him a beer. "I'll be back soon." He walks back to the bedroom.

"He's not around much," she remarks. "And his memory sucks."

"He's not Haley's father?" Olivia asks.

Lydy snorts. "No, that waste of space's been gone for years. No, Dan's just around sometimes, you know how it is. Okay, you two can go!" She points to the door. "I don't care if Haley has a teacher boyfriend. Maybe she'll move the hell out of here and that's good for me."

We stand awkwardly and walk out the door. I turn, about to ask Lydy again to come see Andrea with us, but she slams the door behind us, and I assume she's joining the man in the bedroom.

I look at Olivia as we walk back to her vehicle. My shoulders sag and I sigh. What a letdown. "Well, that was a waste of time. Poor Haley."

Olivia is silent. In fact, she hasn't said much since we arrived here.

I touch her arm. "Are you okay?"

She nods but doesn't say anything. We get into her SUV and pull out back onto the stone lane leading out of the trailer park. She is silent the entire ride home.

Thoughts of our visit with Lydy only an hour earlier fill my mind as I park my car in the parking lot and dash into the pharmacy. I'm worried about Olivia. She barely said goodbye when she dropped me off at my house. A deep sigh escapes me; it's been a long day. I make my way to the back of the store to the prescription pickup counter. Three people stand in front of me, waiting for their pickups. I yawn; it's been a long day and I'm tired. I pull out my phone and start scrolling to kill time while I wait. One person walks away from the counter, only two more to go. Soon it will be my turn. All I want to do is get Emma, go home, take a shower, and eat something.

"Natalie?"

I look up from my phone. Ryan is standing next to me, his dark curly hair recently trimmed, dressed in a smart-looking tan pullover and jeans. He's smiling broadly at me and holding a can of soda.

"Hi, Ryan."

"Picking up a prescription?" he asks. "Dumb question, I guess."

"Yeah, then over to my ex's to pick up Emma. What are you up to?"

"Oh, just had to get some cold medicine."

"Really?" I ask. "You don't look sick."

"Well, basically a sore throat and headache," he replies. "Nothing too terrible, but I wanted to be able to sleep tonight."

"Sure, that makes sense. We all need our sleep. I hope you feel better," I reply.

"Thanks, I'm sure I will." He pauses. "Hey, I've been meaning to call you. I had so much fun when we went out to dinner the other night. Maybe we should plan another night out when you're free."

I study him. Something feels odd here. Ryan doesn't look sick, but he came in for cold medicine at the exact moment I'm here in this exact pharmacy. I like Ryan a lot. We did have a great time when we went out together and I want to plan more dinners, but this feels a bit off for some reason. Thoughts of the strange card I received in the mail the other day populate my mind. I can't imagine Ryan sending that to me, but why is he showing up everywhere I go? Maybe I don't know him as well as I thought.

"Yeah," I say, now moving to the front of the pickup counter line. I tell the pharmacy clerk my name and turn back to Ryan. "I'll call you when I'm free. Good to see you."

I turn away from him to speak to the clerk. When I turn back, he's gone.

THIRTY-FIVE

Him

I sit in my car and wait until she exits the pharmacy. The parking lot is full this time of day and watching the people going in and out with various sized white bags entertains me until Natalie emerges. I have lots of time; no need to rush anything.

I take a drink of my soda, the caffeine gives me the jolt I need, and settle back into my seat. I flick through the photos on my phone, staring at two images I've been consumed with today. I took them the other night when I was inside Natalie's house. One of her, lying peacefully in bed, her full, pouty lips pressed together, and eyes closed, her porcelain-like skin shining with its luminosity even in the darkened room. I swipe to the next photo, the daughter playing Barbies in her room, the newest one, her favorite it seems, riding in the pink car. Then another photo taken right after the earlier one, Natalie sleeping again, this time on the sofa, while the daughter plays with her dolls upstairs, under my watchful eye. This has been fun, slinking around her house, playing tricks, but eventually I know I'll have to get serious.

But I was in the mood for games.
I like being the puppet master.
Pulling her strings.
Until I cut them.

THIRTY-SIX

Olivia

After Lucas leaves for work, I take my coffee into the living room. I place it on the coffee table, plop down in the recliner and pull a blanket up to my chin. A box of tissues sits next to my full coffee mug and that protein shake Lucas made for me, half gone. I try to take another sip of the shake, but my stomach recoils, so I place it down again.

Only a few minutes later, the tears come; not surprising, I'd been holding them in all night. I certainly didn't want Lucas seeing me cry and wonder what was going on. I grab a handful of tissues and blow my nose. I can't hold it inside me for another minute.

So many emotions swirl inside me. Lucas. Haley. Whatever is going on between them. But that isn't the big trigger from yesterday because I already knew those facts. No, it's the visit to Haley's house and speaking to her mother yesterday that I can't stop thinking about.

Seven years ago, at age seventeen, my life was almost exactly like Haley's. I lived in a trailer park with my mom, a muddy road leading around the park—it wasn't even stoned. It was just me and Mom. I hated it. Mom didn't work, but she got a disability check every month from an injury at the factory where she used to work. That check, and food assistance, kept us housed and fed.

My father left when I was three years old, so I have vague memories of him, but nothing substantial. Only that he had dark hair and a nice laugh. After that, a steady stream of various men came and went from our house. Some stayed a few weeks, some several months. I never particularly liked any of them.

Mom wasn't much of a housekeeper. I kept my room tidy, but the rest of the place was usually a mess unless I cleaned it. Same with food. It was hit or miss if our refrigerator held food, or was even switched on or not. As I got older, I did the grocery shopping too; that way I could make sure to buy items that would last us through the month rather than the random food choices my mother always seemed to make and that didn't last very long.

I spent most of my time at my friend's house, Megan, who also lived in the park, just a short walk away. Their trailer was about the same size, but so much different than ours. It was clean, bright and the refrigerator was always full of food. Her mom worked in an office, and I remember how cheerful she was and how well she cared for her daughter and me.

Megan's mom was why I was on the soccer team. Since elementary school, she'd take us to practice, even help me buy uniforms or whatever if my mom wouldn't do it. I was always impressed by her, another single mother with a teenage girl, but she was so different than my mom.

She also warned me about Lucas.

But not my mom.

My mom thought I hit the jackpot, just like Haley's mother. When Megan's mother told mine about Lucas, about him being my soccer coach, what she suspected was going on, my mom was delighted. And then, after a brief period of being happy about my good fortune, she was envious of it.

When Megan died in a car accident shortly after my seventeenth birthday, I lost everything. Megan's mom, Nikki, struggled with the devastating loss of her daughter, and she became increasingly distant from me, until I was completely alone.

My relationship with Lucas was new, maybe a month or so. I'd told Megan about the kisses in the equipment closet, and she must have told Nikki, who then told me to stay away from Lucas. He was too old for me. He would only use me. I think if Megan hadn't died, she would have done more, but after her death, Nikki moved away, leaving me alone with my mother.

Is it any wonder I turned to Lucas then? He filled my days and nights. He was all I wanted. He was all I had. And he promised he'd love me, and care for me, and look after me.

My mom's boyfriend at the time was disgusting, the worst she'd dated. He always leered at me, and I made sure to keep my bedroom door locked at night. I told Lucas about him, and he wanted me to start spending the night at his apartment when the guy was around. Eventually, by the spring of senior year, I was living with him. I owed him so much. Without Lucas, I knew I'd be stuck in that trashy trailer forever, with Mom passed out and that creepy guy moving in on me. Maybe I would have figured a way out on my own, but honestly, I don't know if I would have been strong enough to do it. I think I'm a good person, but I don't have the self-confidence or strength to be on my own, at least that's what I tell myself. I became what Lucas wanted me to be because he was my only option, my view, but maybe I was wrong. I'm sure he recognized this quality in me, and it drew him to me. I would do what he told me.

I was his girl now.

I turned eighteen that spring and in July I married Lucas.

We had only been engaged for a month, but Lucas wanted to marry quickly.

Then we moved in with his mother, far away from Pittsburgh.

And whatever secrets he had there.

We had each other.

And that's all I ever wanted.

Things are different now. I always thought what Lucas and I had was special—it made the beginning of our relationship make sense—but now I wonder was I only one of the many teenage girls he's seduced over the years? Was I special? Has he preyed on vulnerable girls his entire life?

I could barely believe when he kissed me that first time and the subsequent times we met in his locked office. His hands on me, his lips on mine, then his mouth moving down my neck, over my breasts, and between my legs. It was my fantasy come true after all the heart-to-heart conversations we'd had and the closeness that blossomed between us.

I remember lying in my bedroom after one of those late afternoons, stretched out on my twin bed, atop the worn pale pink comforter, and staring at the various posters of rock stars and hunky actors that filled the faded white walls of the space, but I didn't care about them. I had my own rock star.

About two weeks later we had sex. He told me he struggled with our relationship because of our ages and situation, and that made me even more attracted to him. He always thought about me first. Nobody had ever loved me like him. I opened my legs for him that day, but at the same time I opened my heart to him and gave him everything, my trust, my love. I dreamed of this every single moment of every single day since he first kissed me. Feeling him inside me was what I craved, what I wanted, what I knew would eventually happen between us. Afterward, we lay on the couch in his office outside the gym, where he held me close and whispered to me.

"You're my girl now."

I loved hearing those words at the time. I was his and he was mine. We were in love! But those words echoed in my mind throughout the years and instead of making me feel happy and in love, other feelings simmered inside me.

He was thirty-eight years old.

I was barely seventeen.

He was my coach.

But I wanted him so much and this was new territory for him too. He knew it was taboo and that's why he struggled with it too, but something attracted him to me. Something stronger than logic.

Or did he only tell me what I wanted to hear?

I try to bury those feelings though because what does it matter now? We're married, everything is fine, but they still creep inside my thoughts. And now with all of these new revelations, I have serious decisions to make that involve more than myself. The thought of that possibility makes me excited and sad at the same time. I don't think it's what Lucas will want. I don't think he'll be happy about the news.

Other thoughts nip at me about the timeline of our relationship. What we had together was special and unique according to him at the time. He told me he never crossed the line with a student, only me, because he was so drawn to me, and he couldn't help himself. Before he knew it, he was in love with me. He'd had a semiserious relationship in college and when that ended he dated frequently, but nobody special until he met me.

I've been thinking so much about what he told me in the beginning, and I believed every word; he was so convincing. I'm certain now I'm not the first student he crossed the line with; I'm not special, but I was convenient and that's probably why he married me. What if he didn't need me to lie for him that night...? What if he didn't need someone to take care of his sick mother? Would he have discarded me like the others?

He'd been distant with me before everything blew up in Pittsburgh. I lived with him, but we were very vigilant that nobody knew this fact even though I was eighteen by this point and he wasn't technically my coach anymore, as soccer was over for the year. He'd begun saying little things about liking his privacy and not being as attentive as usual, sometimes flat out ignoring me. I thought he might break up with me and that terrified me so when he proposed, shock was my initial response, given his recent behavior. But happiness rang through me, making me oblivious to anything else.

How could I be so stupid?

Now I see marrying me was all about him. The alibi, the caregiver—he needed someone, and I was available. If Lucas hadn't had such needs, I imagine I'd have been discarded years ago.

Like the other girls.

THIRTY-SEVEN

Natalie

The living room is a bit chilly so I close the window I opened earlier. I just checked on Emma and she's sleeping upstairs like an angel with her stuffed bear and frog by her side. I turn on the small gas fireplace, snuggle under a blanket on the sofa and continue to watch a movie while I text with Ryan.

We've been texting a lot the last two days.

I asked him about that note, but he said he didn't send it.

The thought of Ryan lingers in my mind as I wait for his reply. Finally, something pleasant to think about. He mentioned bringing Emma over to meet his new puppy again. My reservations earlier when I saw him at the pharmacy were unfounded. I think I was shaken by the visit with Haley's mother and Olivia's state of mind. I've known Ryan for years, and he's been nothing but a supportive and kind friend. I want to take Emma to meet his new puppy and I think I will, once I get everything sorted out with Lucas and Haley. I think of Ryan's offer to help, but I don't know how he can. The only ones who can stop Lucas are Olivia and myself.

I think Ryan is one of the few good guys, at least he seems to be. He reminds me of Jake in many ways, reliable, giving, kind. We've been friends for a few years, and I genuinely like him. If something more would develop between me and Ryan in the future it would be the first relationship I've had that started with a solid friendship and I think that's a great place to start.

Another text from him pops up.

> My pizza just arrived.

> Sounds good

I hesitate a moment.

> Do you want to bring it over here?

I stare at the three dots until he replies.

> I'd love to. Be there in about fifteen minutes.

I fling off the blanket and hurry into the bathroom, just to give myself a quick once-over. Hair is a bit floppy, but decent. I still have a bit of makeup on, black T-shirt and black leggings. Good enough.

I grab a bottle of Merlot, two wine glasses, a few napkins, two plates, and place them on the coffee table. Then I clear the magazines and books off the table to make room for the pizza box.

I'm excited to see him.

About twenty minutes later, we're sitting on the sofa, biting into some warm, but not hot, pepperoni and sausage pizza and drinking wine.

"Not bad," Ryan remarks, grabbing a napkin to wipe his chin.

"Not bad at all," I reply. "I'm glad I suggested you bring it over."

Ryan laughs. "If I knew bringing pizza over was all I needed to do to see you, I'd have done it sooner."

"Well, I was hungry," I reply. "And we were talking anyway, so it worked."

"What are we watching?"

"A comedy movie." I grab the remote. "I'll restart it so you can watch from the beginning."

We watch the movie, eat pizza, drink wine, and it's just... lovely. A comfortable, fun night spent with someone I enjoy spending time with very much. Nothing dramatic, nothing over the top, just a nice time.

I sneak a look at Ryan when he's laughing at the movie about midway through. I needed a night like this, with someone like him.

He turns to me. "Hey, I was thinking about that note you mentioned to me. Do you mind showing it to me?"

"Um, I actually threw it away," I say. "It was a bit weird, really."

"And you thought I sent it?" His eyebrows rise.

I laugh. "I don't know who sent it. I just thought I'd ask."

He laughs. "I hope you don't think I'm creepy."

I shake my head. "I said weird, not creepy."

"I hope I'm not that either!"

We're both laughing now and it's so fun.

I settle and take another drink of wine. "I'm glad you came over tonight."

Ryan turns to me and grins; his eyes twinkle. "So am I."

THIRTY-EIGHT

Natalie

I watch Haley working with Sam and Dylan at the back table on their division problems. Her hair, smooth, shiny brown, fresh-faced beauty, focused on helping the students understand their problems. After being in her home and meeting her mother, her appearance and work ethic impresses me even more.

Obviously, her mother isn't going to intervene with the relationship between her and Lucas so that leaves it up to me and Olivia. Olivia clammed up on the ride home and didn't answer my text from last night, or tonight. She's probably having second thoughts after yesterday. She's in a different position; Lucas is her husband and despite who he is, I know she loves him—another reason I was so surprised when she wanted to follow him. I feel as if there's much more to Olivia and Lucas's relationship than she's told me.

Haley is such a vulnerable girl, looking for a way out, like I imagine Olivia was even though she never shared her childhood with me. I sense it in the same way Lucas seems to sense vulnerability, only I don't want to take advantage of it. When he sees it in a girl, he knows he can easily infiltrate and consume her entire life. He is all she has to depend on.

I was similar but in a different way. I lived in a typical middle-class house with two parents and a dog, Pepper. We didn't struggle financially, but my parents fought constantly, and it seemed as if they were heading for divorce when I was fourteen. Lucas was a good listener, and I opened up to him about what was going on at home. That was the beginning of a trust between us, a personal connection, that led to him asking if he could kiss me, hold me, eventually leading to a full sexual relationship shortly after I turned fifteen. Everything happened so easily and felt so right at the time. I imagine it was the same for Olivia, and now Haley? Who else has he preyed on in the last twenty years?

I'll call Olivia later; I need to talk to her and then show Andrea those pictures. We'll see how Lucas tries to talk his way out of this one. Now we have proof.

"Mommy, what's for dinner?" Emma asks when we walk into the house after school.

"Hmmm... how about chicken noodle soup and a grilled ham and cheese sandwich?"

"Yum," she says, hanging her backpack on the back of the kitchen chair.

"Any homework tonight?" I ask.

She pulls her handwriting book out of the backpack. "I have to do page three."

I glance at it. "Okay, it's practice for the letter k. This won't take long. Sit at the table and work on it while I start dinner. When you're done, you can play out on your swing set until dinner is ready."

Emma hangs her sweater up on the row of hooks by the

front door, and then settles in on a kitchen chair with her fat yellow pencil. She opens her handwriting workbook and begins to work on her assignment.

I scurry to get the pot of soup I made yesterday onto the stove to warm up and the ingredients for the grilled cheese.

Several minutes pass and then Emma announces, "I'm done!"

I look over her page and her letters look very neat.

"Nice job," I say. "Put it back in your backpack and then you can play."

She hurries over to her backpack, depositing the book inside, and runs outside to play. I turn back to the soup and stir. I go to the refrigerator to retrieve the ham and cheese but type out a quick text to Olivia before assembling the sandwiches.

> Can you talk?

Three dots. Then nothing.

I frown, knowing she read my message. Why isn't she answering?

I go about making dinner but still no answer from Olivia, although Lucas is probably home with her now and maybe she can't talk. She'll probably text me later.

I don't understand Lucas. He's already married to Olivia, who is young and beautiful; you would think he'd be happy with her, not trying to hook up with Haley, risking his marriage, his job, his reputation. It doesn't make any sense to me.

Soon dinner is ready, and Emma and I eat our food. She picks at her sandwich and only eats a few spoonfuls of soup. Something is wrong.

"Are you feeling okay?" I ask.

"Yeah, but I left my sweater at Daddy's house. With the yellow flowers." She sighs. "I want to wear it to school tomorrow."

"We can pick it up tomorrow on the way home from school. You can wear it the next day."

"But Becky's wearing her flower sweater tomorrow. We were going to be twins."

"Oh…" I say. I don't feel like driving over to Jake and Candace's house tonight, but it would probably be easier than listening to Emma moan about it all night. "Okay, I'll text Daddy and see if he's at home. Then we can drive over and pick it up."

"Yay!" Emma's eyes brighten, and she takes a big bite of grilled cheese.

At least this is an easy problem to solve.

Candace said she'd drop off Emma's sweater at our house. She's running out to the grocery store anyway. I finish up the dishes while Emma colors in the living room and watches her cartoons. I put the last dishes in the cupboard and hang up the dish towel just as the doorbell rings.

I open the door. Candace stands on the other side. She's wearing a gray hoodie, jeans and holding Emma's sweater. She smiles at me; it's not a real smile though.

"You're a life saver," I say as she walks inside. "Emma was happy to hear you were dropping it off tonight."

Candace's face lights up. "Was she? Oh, that's great!"

"Would you like a drink, or something?"

"No, I'm off to get groceries," she says, brushing her hair back. "I'll just go say hi to Emma and give her the sweater."

"Oh, okay, she's coloring in the living room."

Candace nods and walks in to see Emma.

"Hi, Candace," Emma says. "My sweater! Thank you!"

Candace lays the sweater on the sofa. "You're welcome, sweetheart," I hear her reply.

Then a pause. I walk to the archway to see Candace pick up Emma's new Barbie from the coffee table.

"I love this doll," she remarks, smiling at the doll and then at my daughter. She stares at it for a few moments. A long time to look at a child's doll.

Weird.

I stay behind the side of the archway and continue to listen.

"Me too," Emma says. "Dad got it for me."

Candace replies in a low voice. I struggle to hear what she says but can't hear her. Then, Emma giggles. Candace whispers something else to her, and Emma smiles, hugging her doll.

"Bye, Emma, have fun at school tomorrow," she says, now in a loud voice. "Will you give me a hug?"

"Yes!" Emma replies.

A couple minutes later, Candace walks back into the kitchen.

"Hey," I say. "What did you say about Emma's doll?"

She stops and stares at me. Not in a particularly friendly way. "I told her it's a pretty doll."

"Oh," I reply, returning her stare. *Like hell you did.* "Well, thanks for bringing the sweater."

"Sure, Natalie." Candace smiles at me and walks out the door.

I don't like that look she gave me. Something strange is going on with her and if it involves Emma, it involves me. I liked Candace initially and thought she would be great for Jake, but now, I'm having some major second thoughts about her.

I mindlessly grab the dishrag in the sink and wipe the kitchen counters. Thoughts pound my brain from all areas, so much so that I'm sure I will soon get a migraine. Olivia, Haley, some weirdo stalking our house, and now this strangeness with Candace. How much can I take? I have answers for none of it.

Emma hums to herself in the next room, and my stomach

lurches. At least she is doing well, but all of these other issues, what am I going to do about them? Everything is stacking up against me and I feel suffocated. I can't handle all of this coming at me at once.

I need a break.

Or else I'm going to crack.

Later that night, I send another text to Olivia. No answer again.

Why is she ignoring me?

I stare at my cell phone, debating if I should call her. I doubt she'd answer, but I have to try. I need to talk to her and tell her everything.

She answers on the second ring.

"I can't talk," Olivia whispers into the phone on the other end.

"Why are you ignoring me?" I ask. "We need to talk. I'm going to show those pictures to Andrea." She's silent on the other end.

"No, you can't..."

"What?" My voice rises. I lower it because I don't want to wake Emma. "We have to do something. Something is going on between them and Haley's mom isn't going to do anything about it, that much is obvious."

"I can't, Natalie. I'm not going to do it anymore."

"Why did you want to follow him in the first place? You know you couldn't trust Lucas," I retort. "He's cheating on you!"

The line is quiet again.

"I'll think about it," Olivia says. "But I can't promise anything."

She hangs up on me.

I lay my phone down on the coffee table. That is so strange. Olivia is the one who started all this business and now she doesn't want to do anything with the information? None of this makes sense. We need to move on this.

I sigh. The visit to Haley's house made my need to intervene between her and Lucas more immediate. Olivia must recognize this too, but why would she suddenly shut everything down now?

I go out to the kitchen to get a snack, selecting a ginger ale and potato chips, not that healthy but who cares. I notice Emma's backpack hanging on the back of the kitchen chair and remember I didn't look at the take-home folder tonight. I grab it and bring it into the living room with my snack. I lay it on the sofa next to me, take a long sip of soda, pop a couple of chips into my mouth, and unzip the bag.

I pull out the folder and a paper on the top falls to the floor. I pick it up; it's a printout that reads...

```
I've been thinking about you for years. Have
    you been thinking about me?
```

My hands shake and I drop the note back to the floor.

THIRTY-NINE

Him

I stretch my legs in the small, confined space clearly designed for children, not adult men. A slight breeze blows a hint of cool air into the structure, and I welcome its arrival.

She'll be here soon.

She usually comes outside to play after dinner.

I try to get here shortly after they arrive home after school, but sometimes I'm late. Luckily, today I'm early to get into my spot. The camera the ex-husband set up has fallen, broken, has been for a couple days and Natalie hasn't noticed. I guess she has a lot going on in her life. I slip in through the broken back fence, the one I broke just for this purpose and others, climb up the wooden steps and into the playhouse attached to the swing set in the backyard.

And I talk to Emma.

We're friends.

Natalie doesn't suspect a thing. She's easy to fool.

The structure is small, but I fit and when Emma climbs up the steps to join me, it's a bit crowded, but it works. She showed me the plastic steering wheel located at the small window and the play binoculars the last time we met.

I hear the patio door open and then slide closed. She's coming out early today. Little feet run across the grass to the rear of the yard, then hurry up the wooden steps to my location.

Here comes my young friend.

Her cute, round face pops up at the top of the steps. She has her long dark hair in pigtails today, each held by a sparkly pink band.

She smiles. "You're here!"

"Hi, Emma," I say in a friendly tone. I hold up the binoculars. "Should we look for scalawags?"

"What's a scalawag?" she asks, her eyes wide. She scrambles into the playhouse and sits on the floor.

"Oh, someone who's up to no good," I explain. "You have to keep a close eye on scalawags."

Emma frowns. "Are *you* a scalawag?"

I laugh. "Some people think I am." I take the play binoculars and look out the small window on the side of the playhouse. "I thought I saw one over by the tree. Here, you take a look."

Emma takes the binoculars and scans the yard.

"Oh, I think I see him! Is he a caterpillar?"

I nod. "He may be. Scalawags come in all shapes and sizes."

She nods, a serious expression on her face, and continues to look through the binoculars. I lean back into the corner, enjoying her having fun. She's a nice kid. Very imaginative and playful.

This is so very fun for me.

I imagine Natalie inside the house right now, clearing dinner off the table, washing dishes, tidying up, thinking her daughter is safely playing in the backyard.

But I'm here.

She's not safe at all.

FORTY

Natalie

I pick the note up again, my hands shaking, and stare at it. The message is obviously intended for me, but to find it in Emma's backpack makes me sick. Lucas must have put it in there at school. A warning to me. I know he wants me to stay away from Olivia. And Haley. I'm the thorn in his side interrupting what he wants to do, and he can't have that; he's Lucas Hanson.

He recognizes me.

He must have told Olivia about our past and that's why she's suddenly acting so strangely. I must talk to her. She's probably mad that I didn't tell her about everything myself. I should have. It's just more reason to shut things down with Haley. Lucas has a pattern of behavior. He's a predator. I'm sure Olivia knows this but isn't ready to admit it.

I sit on the sofa staring at the note and thinking for well over an hour. Then I grab my phone and text Olivia.

> We have to talk.

Nothing.

Then three dots appear. I wait five minutes. Nothing.

> Please Olivia!

Nothing.

I stare at the phone.

She knows and she hates me now. I should have told her the truth. The tears come like a torrent overtaking me. It's the final straw, something as small as a text, but I can't hold it in anymore. Too much is coming at me at once; I need things to slow down.

I need to figure out what to do.

Then a text appears from her.

> He's going out again tonight.

Not what I was expecting; I seize on the opening though and quickly type.

> Do you want to follow him again?

> I can't. Will you?

I stare at the text. Following Lucas is the last thing I want to do. I sigh. I'm not taking Emma with me, but I can ask Brenda next door to stay with her. She's retired, but her husband works night shift and she's up late into the night. She's offered to babysit Emma whenever I need her. Her granddaughter is in fifth grade at school, and I've gotten to know Brenda quite well in the short time we've lived here.

> Yes. Are you okay?

She doesn't answer.

. . .

I slink across the back parking lot near the cafeteria and enter the small, wooded area surrounding the school playground. The tote bag containing the camera hangs on my shoulder.

Instead of parking outside Lucas's house for half an hour, waiting for him to leave, I should have just waited at my house. He met Haley at the school; I guess it's where he feels powerful, where he can play out his sick fantasies. Then the two of them walked up the grassy area to the playground. He's pretty bold choosing the school to meet her, but he's not totally stupid. I know why he leads her to the playground rather than staying by the car.

No cameras.

Cameras are positioned at every entrance point, but none by the swing sets and sliding boards. Lucas knows this.

I position myself among the trees and adjust the zoom. Moonlight streams through the trees as I watch them hold hands on the swing. I snap a few photos and wait for more. I'm certain more will develop between them tonight. I crouch lower to the ground, thankful for the secrecy of the foliage. I wonder what Olivia is doing now; I'm not sure why I agreed to follow him again. I feel like a lunatic crouched in the bushes.

They're still holding hands, smiling, and talking intimately. An old memory plays in my mind. A park Lucas and I used to go, to walk, talk, make out. I know what Haley's feeling right now, and my heart aches for Olivia when she sees these pictures.

I'm a stalker lurking around in the dark, crouching low, poised with my camera. This whole situation is so ridiculous, and it's absolutely the last time I'm doing this, even if Olivia asks again.

Lucas and Haley are moving now. They pause by the sliding board and Lucas kisses her and when he does her arms go around his neck. He kisses her again and eases her onto the sliding board, his hands now unbuttoning her shirt.

Adrenaline pulses through me. Oh, more is happening tonight!

I zoom and snap. Zoom and snap.

Then I place the camera back into the tote bag. I can't lurk in the darkness watching this unfold.

I'm going to stop it.

I step out of my hiding spot to confront Lucas, but something else is happening now. Haley is sitting up on the sliding board and buttoning her shirt. She puts her hand up and it looks like she's telling him to stop.

He stops and the two stand up. I step back into my hiding spot. I watch them talk for a few minutes and then walk back to their cars and drive away.

I pat my tote bag containing my camera and the photographs inside it. Now we have proof Lucas can't deny. A little feeling of satisfaction washes over me.

You're done, Lucas Hanson.

FORTY-ONE

Natalie

The next morning my nerves are frazzled. I pour two bowls of cereal for breakfast, and Emma and I sit down at the kitchen table. A soft rain patters on the roof and I enjoy its soothing sound and make a mental note to take an umbrella today to school. I take a sip of orange juice, but my mind is somewhere else.

Maybe Lucas doesn't know who I am now, maybe the note is from someone else; and is Olivia angry at me? I texted her late last night about what I saw on the playground, but she never responded. She still hasn't talked to me other than asking me to follow Lucas. All of this has gone on long enough. I'm sick of Lucas thinking he can do whatever damn thing he wants to do without any repercussions. I'm going to stop it *now*!

"I want to be a fairy princess for Halloween," Emma is saying between bites of cereal. "We have a parade at school and a party in our classroom!"

"Oh, I know. That will be fun," I reply. Halloween is next

week; I better get busy finding her a costume. I'll probably have to make something for the party too. "Did you sign up to bring anything for the party?"

"Brownies," she says.

I continue to eat my cereal, listening to Emma talk about Halloween and trying to push my worries away. At least the regular school routine will be safe. Hopefully I'll have a normal day and we will go from there. I'll only interact with Lucas when it involves my students, same as I've been doing since the beginning of the school year. I will ignore the note and everything for now. I stand up to retrieve the envelope of photographs from my desk drawer in the living room. I reach in, but I don't see the envelope. I know I put them in there. I'm sure of it. I need those pictures to show Andrea, or the whole situation could turn on me, and Lucas will easily spin it as me being obsessed with him again.

Where are those photographs? I can print new ones, but not now.

"Mommy, I'm done," Emma says. "It's time to go to school."

I nod, clear our breakfast dishes away and deposit them into the dishwasher thinking about what I need to do. I will print out new photos of Lucas and Haley and go to Andrea with those to discuss. When I get home I will print out the ones of them on the sliding board, but I need to discuss those with Olivia before showing Andrea. And I will continue to text and call Olivia. I have to talk to her.

I also need to find a good brownie recipe and a fairy princess costume. I sigh.

Time for school.

The morning passes at a snail's pace and by the time lunchtime rolls around my stomach is in knots. Why am I so nervous about showing those photos to Andrea? I printed new ones on my classroom copier. They aren't the best quality, but they will work. I barely drink my water and choke down a few crackers, hoping it will settle my rumbling stomach. I've given up eating in the faculty room, preferring to take my lunch at my desk and enjoy the short period of quiet in my busy day. But today I'm antsy and I need to do something. Haley is out sick today so it's only me. Only me and Lucas. I have a few minutes before I head down to his room, so I walk over to the kindergarten hallway to say hi to Emma and talk to her teacher, Cathy Frasier, for a few minutes.

Emma is at the blue table in the center of the room working on cutting out different color fish from a worksheet. I walk over to the table.

"Hi, Emma," I say.

"Mommy! Oh, Mom," she corrects herself. I guess she doesn't want to sound like a baby in front of her friends. Losing the title of Mommy puts a little stab to my heart, but that's okay, it's part of growing up.

I smile. "What are you working on?"

She holds up the worksheet. "My colors."

"Looks great. I just stopped in to say hello. I'm going to talk to Mrs. Frasier for a moment."

"Bye, Mom," Emma says, going back to her cutting.

Cathy Frasier is by the SMART Board, typing on her laptop at the standing desk located at the side of the board. She looks up and smiles at me.

"Hi, Natalie," she greets.

"Hi, Cathy." I return her smile. "Just saying a quick hello to Emma."

"Oh, she's such a sweet girl," replies Cathy.

"Thank you," I say. "Well, I'm off to fourth grade. Lucas Hanson's class."

Cathy's smile widens. "Oh, Lucas. He was in here

yesterday reading a book to the class during his prep period. The kids love the funny voices he makes when he reads. He gets so into the characters."

My ears perk up. "Oh, really?"

"Yeah, he does that every so often. He's such a great guy. Really something."

"He's really something," I mumble. I say goodbye and walk down the hall to Lucas's room.

I travel slowly down the hall, not wanting to reach my destination.

I stop at the office to check my mailbox, then use the bathroom, anything to postpone reaching Lucas's room.

But then I arrive at his door.

Inside, the students are in small clusters at the back table, on the floor, and some at their desks.

"Ah, Mrs. Amaryllis," Lucas greets me. His face smiles, but his eyes do not.

"Mr. Hanson," I reply.

"The students are reviewing for the test. Another ten minutes and we'll start."

"Okay, do you have my students' tests?"

"Sure." I follow him to his desk and stare at him as he rifles through a stack of papers on his desk. He looks through papers on the other side of the desk. "Odd, I thought I had them here."

I stare at him sorting through the papers on his desk. Did he leave the note in Emma's backpack? I thought there would be a bit of a confrontation between us when I walked into his room, but while he doesn't appear happy to see me—no surprise there —it doesn't seem as if anything has changed. Surely, if he recognized me, he'd say so. Then I glance at his laptop, sitting next to the papers. There's a WhatsApp conversation open on the screen; a photo is the latest message.

"Oh, here they are." Lucas grabs the stack of tests from the filing cabinet behind his desk and gives me three of them.

I barely hear him through the sudden ringing in my ears. Heat floods my body, and my mouth goes dry. I clutch the stack of tests and proceed to the door, but the photo is still clear in my mind. My face flushes and anger rises inside me. Damn it, not again!

A photo of a positive pregnancy test.

FORTY-TWO

Natalie

I hurry down the hall to my classroom, students and tests in tow, but my movements are a blur; only one thought occupies my mind. The pregnancy test.

A *pregnancy* test!

How did I allow it to go this far?

I tell the students to sit down at their desks and start on the test and to raise their hand if they have any questions. I sit down at my desk. Normally I'd read the test aloud to them, but luckily this test is mostly division and graphs, so I don't need to do so. I don't know if I can at this point, I'm so distracted.

I stare at my inbox sitting in front of me, still seeing the image of the positive pregnancy test in my mind.

Just like me.

Lucas has ruined Haley's life, just like mine, and now he will walk away and act like he barely knows her anymore, letting her handle the knowledge she is going to have their baby.

Alone.

He won't answer her repeated calls and texts. He won't

interact with her at all anymore, and she will be devastated. Thoughts of our recent visit to her home flood my mind; she's not going to have any type of support with her mother. She's going to be on her own completely.

Sure, she could press charges, sue him for child support, but she won't, because she'll believe it's only a phase. He's made her feel so special, told her he loved her, and he must still feel that way. He will love her again. And she can't damage his reputation; he's already warned her of that, their relationship must always remain a secret. Of course he will still love her. She's his girl. That's what he's told her all these months they've been together.

No, he won't.

Tears form in my eyes, but I will them away. I will not cry.

He won't even talk to her. She'll be the one who makes all the decisions for the baby.

If she's allowed.

I wasn't even allowed to do that.

I struggle through the evening, but I get everything done. I'm glad Emma and I ran our errands quickly after school today. I didn't go to Andrea with the photos; I want to talk to Olivia before I do. I tried to call Olivia, no answer. I emailed her the new pictures from the playground. No response. Dinner, homework, and coloring with Emma, bathtime, bedtime book—and finally, she's peacefully asleep in her twin bed with a soft, pink comforter and her treasured stuffed bear and frog. She's healthy, safe, and with me, exactly where she should be, where she belongs.

A sob rises in my throat, and I quickly exit Emma's room before it escapes. I hurry downstairs to the sofa, grab a handful of tissues from the box and quietly let it out.

Tears stream down my face and I let them. I've held them in

for too long. I haven't thought about him in years. I lie: I think about him every day. Every day for the last twenty years.

My baby boy.

My relationship with Lucas started shortly after my fifteenth birthday; he bought me a dozen red roses for my birthday and took me out to dinner and dazzled me in every way. We broke up seven months later. I was pregnant, and he wanted nothing to do with me. I couldn't believe how he went from daily calls and texts, meeting secretly after school in his coach's office, to absolutely nothing. Soccer was over for the season, but he also coached track, so the coach's office continued to be our usual meeting place. He didn't want me coming to his apartment; he had a roommate and thought it wasn't a good idea. Yeah, probably not since I was *fifteen*. He was acting like he barely knew me, even though I held his baby inside my body. He was so distant, cold, heartless.

I didn't know what to do so I told my parents. I told them I was dating a boy but he moved away and we had already broken up. Lucas had routinely reminded me our relationship had to always remain a secret. Even though he was giving me the cold shoulder, I didn't want to disappoint him. I loved him and I thought he still loved me. He had to. I still loved him. I believed every single word he said to me.

My parents took control of the situation and made things easy for Lucas. My dad had a job opportunity in Pittsburgh, and we moved there when I was two months pregnant. They pressured me hard to get an abortion, but I didn't want to; I couldn't. I wanted this baby so I agreed to adoption, but hoped once the baby arrived, they would change their minds.

They didn't and they made it clear that if I decided to keep the baby I'd have no support system. I'd be completely on my own. I was sixteen. I had no idea how to live on my own. So, I did what they wanted me to do, even though it's not what I wanted at all. I gave my baby up for adoption and have regretted it every day of my life. My son would be twenty years old now. I have no idea what he looks like, where he lives, what he likes to do or if he's happy.

The only thing I know is that I love him.

I wipe the tears away. I can't do anything about him, only say a prayer for him, for his safety and his happiness, as I have done for the last twenty years. But I can do something about Lucas and Haley. He will be responsible for their baby. I will make sure of it.

I grab my phone to text Olivia...

> Something else has happened.

She responds immediately.

> What?

> Come over and I'll tell you.

I wait ten minutes for her response.

> Okay, I'll be there soon. Lucas just fell asleep. I want to make sure he's out.

I lay the phone down and rise from the sofa, wiping my face one more time before tossing the tissues in the kitchen trash. But the trash can isn't in its usual spot by the refrigerator. Instead, it sits by the front door. I struggle to remember moving it, but I don't think I did. We went to a drive thru for fast food tonight for dinner, no way I was cooking, and I remember throwing the trash in the can and it sat in its usual spot.

A chill runs up my spine.

Has someone been in my house while I was upstairs with Emma?

I look at the door, securely deadbolted. I go back to retrieve my phone to look at the camera feed. An Amazon delivery, but that's the only person, other than Emma and myself. I check the camera feed by the back door, but there's only a few minutes of video, nothing unusual, but then it goes black. What happened to the camera?

I shiver again, a coldness coming from the living room. Then I remember opening one of the windows when Emma and I were coloring because it was so hot in the room. I hurry over to the window by the recliner. It's only open a quarter of the way, just as I had left it, but could someone have sneaked in and, what, moved my trash can? Why the hell would someone do that?

I'm losing my mind. I can't take any more of this.

I seriously can't take one more thing being thrown at me!

I shake my head. Emma must have moved it for some reason. I close the window, go back to the kitchen, move the trash can back, and deposit my tissues.

There's a soft knock on the door; I open it and Olivia walks inside.

She looks terrible. It's obvious she's been crying too. She's incredibly pale and, if possible, thinner than the last time I saw her, which was only a few days ago. She looks like she hasn't slept well either, judging by the dark circles under her eyes. She shoves her hands into the pockets of the dark green sweater she wears.

"I'm here," she says flatly. She looks at me. "Were you crying?"

"Yes," I admit. "Let me put some water on for tea. I think we'll need it."

FORTY-THREE

Olivia

The TV is droning on some news channel Lucas had on before he left for work. I grab the remote and switch to a home decorating show to distract me. I watch the kitchen remodel on the screen while drinking the remainder of my protein drink Lucas made me before he left for work. I sit the glass down on the coffee table and rub my stomach.

My phone beeps with an incoming text. It's from her again, Diana. I read it and stare at the picture she attached. My heart sinks at the photo of a pretty brunette smiling at the camera. It's the necklace she's wearing around her neck that causes my reaction.

A familiar necklace.

I jump off the sofa and hurry into Lucas's office. I open the left drawer of his desk in the center of the room and retrieve the key in the back. I walk over to the safe in the corner of the room and unlock it. I sort through the stack of papers, looking for the small manilla envelope I remember seeing a few years ago when we were going through his mother's paperwork.

It lies under the stack of papers.

I pull it out, open it, and allow the contents to fall to the floor. Lying on the oak hardwood floor is a silver Celtic knot pendant necklace with an emerald heart in the center.

The first time I saw it Lucas told me it was his mother's and it was sentimental to him. Now I know it was Angie's. Diana said she wore it every day, but it was never recovered after her murder. This necklace was a symbol to Diana's sister, a symbol of finding her strength again and rediscovering herself.

And he took it.

Off her dead body.

I run back to the sofa, gripping the necklace, and take a picture of it with my phone. I text it to Diana with a message.

> I'm sorry I didn't believe you. I found your sister's necklace in Lucas's safe. I believe you now.

I toss the phone down and stare at the necklace.

My husband is a murderer.

Later that night, I watch Lucas pace the floor in our kitchen. Around the kitchen table, past the china hutch, over to the small island in the center of the room, back around the kitchen table while I finish heating the grilled chicken for our salads.

"I don't want you to be friends with her," he is saying. "I don't know what her problem is with me, but she definitely has one! There's just something about her that I can't quite place my finger on."

I shake my head. "I don't understand why you're so upset."

Lucas sighs. "Of course not, but I'm telling you, I think she's obsessed with me, and you."

I sigh, listening to his ridiculous tirade. He's been ranting on about Natalie for twenty minutes and I'm sick of it. What about him being a *murderer*! What about murdering Angie! And funny how he barely mentions Haley, other than to say he's only paying more attention to her to help her learn about becoming a teacher. I mention the heart with his name scribbled inside, but he scoffs it off as silly, yet I notice the hint of a smile that crosses his face when I mention it. Oh, he likes it. He wants her; I know that. But he continues to tell me all about how he's instructing her on different teaching methods. He's a born mentor. Those are his words, not mine.

Shut up, Lucas.

The chicken sizzles and I turn off the stove. I put the chicken on top of our already prepped salads, and we sit down to eat. I spear some lettuce and put it in my mouth as I stare at my husband at the other end of the table doing the same. I add a bit of salad dressing, then stare at the flickering flameless candles in the center of the table lending an almost romantic feel to the space, but I'm feeling anything but romantic. Lucas continues ranting about Natalie between bites, but I tune him out and just stare at him. I love looking at him; I always have. His good looks make life easy for him, easy to flirt and maneuver other people's lives. He has many admirable skills and qualities but love and loyalty are not on that list. He's a user. Not of drugs or alcohol, but a user of people.

After my conversation with Diana today, none of my loyalties lie with Lucas. I'm on Natalie's side. Not that she knows. She's freaking out, I know, but I need time. To think, consider, and decide. Strange how Natalie, whom I've only known a couple of months, can see past Lucas's mask to the true person inside. I knew there was a reason I was so drawn to her the minute I met her at the school carnival. There's something special about her, although I didn't know what it was at the time; now I do.

She sees what I see.

She knows.

I don't have to pretend with her.

I'm not alone anymore.

Lucas is staring at me now. His dark eyes waiting for me to answer. I take a long sip of water, keeping my gaze on him.

"What?" I ask, placing the glass back down on the table.

"What? Are you even listening to me?" he demands. Anger flashes in his eyes.

"You have a problem with Natalie for some reason."

"No, she has a problem with me for no reason! That's the problem. You'd know that if you'd listen," he growls.

I cock my head. "You seem like the one obsessed."

Now he's mad. He glares at me. "Really, that's what you think."

"When have you ever cared about what I think?" My boldness surprising me. "When have you cared about anyone else other than yourself? What about that girl at the bar in Pittsburgh? Did you care about her? Care that she died!"

He pushes away from the table and jumps up. He puts his hands tightly against my arms, squeezing, and is in my face. Barely an inch away. "Don't ever talk about that. You know we *never* talk about that. You promised. You know I'm innocent. I just made a bad decision getting into a fight with that guy. That's it."

My boldness is gone, and I shake, but I don't cry, and he lets go of my arms, then storms off. I shouldn't have mentioned Angie. I need to make a plan before I confront Lucas with what I know, and my first move is to change the locks when he's at school tomorrow. My phone buzzes inside my jeans pocket. I pull it out, a missed call from the Natalie. A text pops up from her.

Check your email.

I quickly delete the call and text because Lucas sometimes

looks at my phone. And then I pull up my email. There are four pictures of Lucas and Haley. It looks like they are on a playground. They are swinging, side by side, in one, holding hands walking by the basketball court, and finally, lying on a slide, Lucas on top of her, kissing Haley and unbuttoning her shirt. Natalie said it was the school playground at midnight last night, shortly after I texted her about him going out.

Fucking asshole.

He's never going to change.

Even though I knew it was true, seeing the evidence makes me sick and disgusted at him and myself for believing his lies all these years. I should have known better. If I think about it, really think about it, he didn't try that hard to hide it from me, but I didn't see it at first. Or did I see it and hide it away from myself because I didn't want to believe it was true?

FORTY-FOUR

Olivia

Lucas falls asleep early. I guess he was worn out from all his action on the sliding board last night. We haven't talked at all since the confrontation at dinner. I don't know if I ever want to talk to him again. I stare at him sleeping soundly on the sofa, a soft cotton blanket covering him. One thing is for sure, this is the last time he's going to do this to me. I'm not going to put up with this anymore.

I need to talk to Natalie.

It's as if she knows I'm thinking about her because another text from her pops up on my phone, and I'm soon on my way to her house, after a few minutes of watching Lucas sleep on the sofa; I want to make sure he's out for the night.

When I walk inside and she takes one look at me and says she's making tea, I realize how bad I must look.

And she doesn't look much better.

I nod and sit down at the kitchen table. A bag of Double Stuf Oreos sits beside me. I open it and take one, gobbling it down.

Natalie turns away from the stove as the kettle heats the water and her eyes widen, then smiles at me.

"Take two, or three," she says, grabbing one herself. "They're delicious."

Natalie sits down and looks at me sympathetically. "Haley's pregnant."

"What?" I yell. Is she serious? Haley's *pregnant* with Lucas's baby?

"Shh... Emma's sleeping," she says. "I saw a photo on Lucas's laptop today. I'm so sorry, Olivia, it was a positive pregnancy test."

I chuckle, momentarily relieved. "That was me. I'm pregnant."

Natalie stares at me, dumbfounded. "Oh..."

"Is that the only reason you thought Haley was pregnant?"

"Yes, but, Olivia, this is big news. You're pregnant?"

"Yes, I know." I let out a deep sigh. I've still not begun to process the idea. "It's what I've wanted for so long, but now with everything going on with Lucas, it just feels like so much."

Natalie nods. "It's a lot. How did Lucas take the news?"

"He hasn't said much about it. He wanted a photo, proof," I say sadly.

Natalie nods. "I'm sorry about that, but I'm happy for you."

I nod but I don't want to think about this anymore, so I pull out my phone and click on the photos she sent me earlier.

"I'm so sorry, Olivia. I hated sending those pictures to you, but you had to see them," she says, giving me a hug. "I thought it was true, but now we know for sure."

"Yeah, I'm realizing he's not the person I thought he was," I reply. "You know, I thought Lucas and I could be the perfect family with the baby. I've been so naive for all these years. I believed what he told me, but now I see his lies. He's that selfish. That's why I pulled away from you. But I knew I was lying to myself. Then I saw those pictures tonight."

Natalie nods. "I understand."

I grab another cookie. "He's never going to change," I repeat. Mostly for myself because I need to understand that fact and the big change my life will now take as I separate myself from him. There's just so much information to process right now.

The whistle on the kettle sounds, and Natalie hurries to move it off the burner. She gets the tea ready as I continue to talk.

"There's more about Lucas that I haven't told you," I say. "We didn't get married because we were so in love. Well, I was, but I don't think he was, but I lied for him. I believed he was innocent."

She turns around. "You lied?"

"Um... yes." I still hesitate to tell her what happened.

"Honey or sugar?" she asks.

"What?"

"For the tea."

"Oh, honey."

She brings the tea over, and we each sip the hot comfort in silence.

"Do you want to tell me?"

I look at her and nod. "Yes, I want to tell you everything."

I pause again and spill my story. "Six years ago, I was dating Lucas for about a year. I just turned eighteen, but I'd been living with him for about six months. I had... a similar home life to Haley when I was growing up and that's another reason I was so freaked out after our visit there. And it's why I felt so grateful to Lucas for getting me out of there and giving me a better life, although I now see he did it for himself, not me. Anyway, we were living in Pittsburgh, and one night he came home really late, stinking of alcohol and smoke. I knew he had been at a bar or something. He showered and went to bed, but then I got up to look in the hamper. His shirt had dried blood all over it.

Then, the next day the dirty clothes he wore the night before were missing from the hamper. He told me he had gotten into a fight with a guy, given him a bloody nose, but that a girl was killed at the bar that night too. Police thought him and this guy he got into a fight with had killed her. He begged me to tell the police he was home with me, which I did. There's no way I thought he would have hurt that girl..." I stop, fiddling with the cookie package in front of me.

"Go on," Natalie says.

"The girl, her name was Angie, she knew Lucas from when she was in high school."

"Let me guess, he was her soccer coach," she says. "And she was in a relationship with him."

"Yes, for two years during her junior and senior years. This was at the school he taught at before coming to my school. He broke it off with her when she graduated, but now she wanted everyone to know he was a predator and how he manipulated her when she was a minor. She told her family, got a lawyer, and was going to make a formal complaint against Lucas the following week."

"She was murdered the week before she was going to make the complaint, wow."

I nod. "She was found in the alley behind the bar. She was stabbed..."

"And they thought it was Lucas?"

"The family did, but the police had no real evidence. The girl was seen talking in the bar to a guy, a criminal according to the police. He had been arrested before for robbery and assault, and they arrested him for it. But the police did question Lucas. And I gave him an alibi saying he had been home with me the entire night."

"Had he?"

I shake my head. "After school I worked at my part-time job

and got back to his apartment around eight thirty. He wasn't there. He got home after midnight."

"Why did you lie for him?"

My eyes well up with tears. "I loved him. And I trusted him; I really thought he was innocent." My voice wavers. "But not anymore."

"You think he killed her?" Natalie asks. "What changed your mind?"

"Not at the time. I never thought he killed anyone. If I had, I wouldn't have lied for him. I truly thought he was innocent. But... the girl's sister, Diana, sent Lucas a letter a few weeks ago accusing him of the murder. She saw the article about him being Teacher of the Year. She'd just moved to this area and was disgusted that he got away with her sister's murder. I opened the letter and I've been talking to her, but I didn't believe her at first. Then she sent a picture of her sister Angie and the necklace she wore in the picture..."

"Yes?" Natalie stares at me.

"The necklace was never recovered after her murder, and Diana said she wore it every day. And I saw that necklace before. Lucas has the exact necklace locked in his safe." I pause. "I think he killed her."

"What!" Natalie exclaims.

I nod. "All of this is crazy. I've been so oblivious to who he really is. I mean, I loved him and I only wanted to marry him and be with him. I was only worried about him being all mine and that's all I wanted."

"And now it's all coming back, and you regret your decision," Natalie says. "But you didn't know he was a murderer, and you didn't realize how he was lying to you. He's very gifted at manipulating people."

"I do and I don't; it's complicated." I pause. "I felt guilty lying, but I didn't want to go back to live with my mother and her creepy boyfriend, and I never could have imagined he could *kill* someone!"

Natalie sighs, popping another cookie in her mouth. "You felt trapped; I can understand that feeling. Well, it's about to get a lot more complicated. I should have told you this sooner. I met Lucas years ago, in high school, just like you and Angie..."

And she tells me.

I sit in the car outside Natalie's dark house; it's past one in the morning and she was going straight to bed after I left. As I dwell in the quiet car, I wonder if I want to go home. Right now, I don't even feel like I have a home; everything is so messed up I don't know what to do next. The one consolation I have is Natalie's friendship. She's a single mother and doing such a great job with Emma; I know I can do the same and I'm comforted by knowing Natalie will be there to help me along. I value her friendship so much.

It's so strange that Natalie and I had the same experiences with Lucas. Even her story about the first time he kissed her in the equipment closet is the same as mine. It's disgusting how he knows how to seduce young women so methodically and has used the same scenarios over and over again, like he was reading from a script. My heart broke for her when she told me how it ended, his cold distance, and everything she gave up. My time is ending with Lucas too, but I will still have my baby.

A movement catches my eye behind me. I look into the rearview window. A figure, appearing to be a man, dressed in a black hoodie, pulled up over his head, and jeans walks on the sidewalk across the street at the school, heading toward the playground in the back of the building.

What the fuck?

Is it Lucas, meeting Haley again?

I grab my phone. No messages from him. Surely, he noticed I was gone when he got up to go on his little rendezvous. Unless he thought I went to sleep in the extra bedroom like I do if he snores too much. Or after our fight, he doesn't give a hoot where I am. So, now he thinks it's a good idea to meet an underage girl for a late-night make-out session? Who the hell does he think he is?

Fury builds inside me. Fury at Lucas. Fury at myself for being so oblivious to what is right in front of me. Ugh... he always treats me like I'm incapable of making decisions for myself. Eat healthy, drink water, it's the fountain of youth, do this, do that, all for him. What about me?

Fuck the fountain of youth.

I hate that stupid phrase.

I hate him.

I open the car door, close it, and run across the street. The hooded man, probably my husband, is clipping away, now almost at the end of the sidewalk about to step onto the grass to meet his high school lover. I sprint and yell.

"You!"

I'm pointing at him now. He glances back but the hood and shadows still obscure his face. He turns and runs into the grass.

"You better run!" I scream, now running as fast as I can. I quickly reach the end of the sidewalk, panting now. I stop for a moment to survey the area, and I see him enter the grove of trees at the side of the playground. I run across the basketball court and see him scramble again, running across the yards to the neighboring house and disappearing from my view.

I double over, gasping for breath now. My breathing slows and my body calms. I look around the playground again, expecting to see Haley somewhere, but the only one here is me.

The moon hangs high in the sky tonight and the black tapestry surrounding it is brightened by twinkling stars. I trudge over to the swing set, giving the sliding board some side eye as I pass it, and plop on the swing. I push my legs on the ground, and it lifts me higher and higher into the sky. If Haley's not here, I guess that wasn't Lucas.

Who did I just chase away?

FORTY-FIVE

Him

I watch her and I gather information during the time inside and outside of her home, but it's not enough. I need to get what I want, my whole reason for all these cloak-and-dagger games. Sure, it's fun but I have a mission, a goal. Hiding Natalie's bathrobe isn't getting me there. But watching her scurry around and wonder about its location did give me a sick thrill.

I am a bit sick.

In the head.

Now she changed the locks and didn't leave an extra under the planter, so I don't have the luxury of entering whenever I please. Luckily, Natalie is forgetful about leaving a window open and on occasion I can slip in that way.

And why is Olivia always with her? I watch them and listen to their boring conversations sometimes. Again, Natalie's habit of leaving the windows open in the living room and the kitchen allows me to slither between the bushes for a listen. Seems like Olivia is always here on those nights I lie among the shrubbery. On and on and on... blah blah blah. How much tea can those two women drink every time they talk? I'm tired of her too. I'm not even bothered when Natalie closes the window shortly after Olivia arrives, even though I'm in a comfortable spot in the shrubbery under the window. All they do is bitch and complain, a real bore.

I'm going to snap soon, but she keeps telling me to wait, that it's not the right time. Damn it to hell, it is the right time! No, I will tell *her* when it's the right time. We have some history, but I can't be at her beck and call forever. She is helpful, and I'm thankful for that aspect, but things are going to change very soon.

A man's gotta do what a man's gotta do.

FORTY-SIX

Natalie

One thing I don't tell Olivia about is Theo. I never tell anyone about him, of course, but maybe I should have made an exception in this case. My mind can barely wrap itself around what she just told me. What are the chances of Theo and Lucas having an involvement with the same girl in Pittsburgh that was murdered, Angie? It must be the same girl. It's almost unbelievable, but as outlandish as it is, I understand how the pieces fit together now, and that's helpful in a way, though not necessarily a relief. The old phrase "It's a small world" certainly is relevant in this case. Olivia lied for Lucas to keep him safe and with her. I framed Theo to keep him away from me and in jail. But I now know that means I helped Lucas walk free.

Those are the facts.

I'm lying in my bed staring at the ceiling. I hear a noise outside and listen more closely. I think it's only a car door closing, probably Olivia. This was a night of revelations that shocked us both. And all the stories revolve around one man.

One man who does whatever the fuck he wants to do and doesn't give a fuck about the women he destroys in his path.

Lucas Hanson.

Lucas may have killed someone. This news shocks me—I never saw him as a murderer—and running over the details that Olivia shared with me in my mind, I'm still in shock. As much as I don't trust him, know he's a controlling, manipulating person, I never imagined he could kill someone.

He's more dangerous than I thought.

My thoughts drift back to the note I found in Emma's backpack. I thought Lucas was just trying to scare me to show he's one step ahead of me and I couldn't win against him. Nobody will believe anything negative I'd have to say about him since he's so beloved in the school.

But the note may have more sinister intentions. Nerves creep through my body at the possible implications for me and for Emma. Are we in danger now? I don't even know if it came from Lucas; I'm sure if it was him, he would have said something to me today about recognizing me. I know he would.

Who put the note in Emma's backpack?

Unless Lucas is playing games with me, luring me into a false sense of security thinking that he doesn't recognize me.

I don't have any answers.

I printed out some larger, high-definition pictures at the custom photo lab located next to the pharmacy. Emma and I stopped there right after school. And tomorrow I will show Andrea. I already checked if it was okay with Olivia, and she agreed. Although I have reservations about showing them to Andrea—even though I know it's something I need to do with this new knowledge about Lucas. I may be putting myself and Emma in physical danger. I try to think of all the possibilities and solutions that will keep me and Emma safe, but it's endless.

I don't know what he will do.

I don't know what will happen.

And what about all the odd occurrences around the house? Could Lucas be sneaking into my house and doing these weird things? Would he really do that? I need to think carefully about what I will do and how I will do it to keep Emma and myself safe. I'm dealing with a much more unstable person than I realized. I never truly considered I could be in danger from Lucas. I feared the mental games he'd play, that he would destroy me professionally, but knowing that he'd kill to keep his secret is a whole other level. And Olivia, she's been living with a murderer for years... and is still living with him. I have to help her too.

This is why I haven't been open to any new relationships. Who has worse taste in men than me? Criminals, rapists, and murderers, I really know how to pick them. What is wrong with me? I like to see the good in people and I guess I ignore the bad qualities until they can't be ignored. It's funny, the characteristic both Lucas and Theo share is charisma. That flash of excitement and danger that I was instantly attracted to—that's what I need to avoid. Instead, I want steady and safe, comfortable—not boring, but a real connection with someone who truly cares about me.

I roll over in bed, wanting to quiet my brain, but too much spins inside it, too much to think about, too much to worry about, too much of everything. I only want silence.

But none ever comes.

Shadows dance on my bedroom ceiling, a mix of the moonlight and the occasional car passing by on the nearby road. I went to bed over an hour ago and sleep still eludes me.

I think about him as I have on many sleepless nights. My son. I held him briefly after birth. He had a head of dark hair and a strong set of lungs, but in those few moments he was calm, peaceful, and mine.

I named him Andrew. If I were allowed to keep him, I'd have called him Drew. I always loved that name.

A few minutes later, he was taken from me and given to his adoptive parents. He was gone and I'd never see him again, even though he was a part of me. And at the time a result of the love I thought I shared with Lucas.

My life continued in a strangely normal pattern after his birth. I went to a new high school where nobody knew anything about my past. I was just a normal, carefree teenager and I relished that normalcy. I studied hard, joined student council and yearbook, and went out on dates. My parents were delighted. Their daughter was back, her troubled past now nonexistent.

But at night, I lay in my bedroom staring at the ceiling, like tonight, and I thought of Drew. Does he have pudgy cheeks now? Is he smiling? What foods does he like? What does his laugh sound like? I have cried myself to sleep so many nights and then I'd wake in the morning, wash my tear-streaked face, get dressed, and go about my day while my heart was shattered in a million jagged pieces piercing me every single day.

Some nights were different. Nights I called Lucas's cell number over and over again, but he never answered. I left messages, sent texts, begging him to call me just to talk. I didn't even know what I wanted to say to him. My heart ached at losing Drew, but also of losing what I thought I had with Lucas. One day he was kissing me, winking at me during soccer practice when the other girls weren't watching, and telling me how much he loved me.

I was his girl.

Then I was nothing.

Our baby was nothing.

I didn't understand how any of it happened. It felt like a nightmare every single night. After seeing that photo on his laptop today, it brought back those feelings of agony I had for so long.

Drew is a grown man now. Does he look like me or Lucas? I hope he's a good man, like Jake, not like Lucas. I often have the thought I may meet him in passing, at the grocery store or the movies. Surely, I'd know my own son. I'd recognize him; but more so I'd feel the connection, I'm certain of it.

I roll over on my side and bury my head in the pillow, tears staining the cool cotton. Tomorrow, I will get up, get dressed, and conduct my day as normal, but, tonight, as so many nights, I will cry myself to sleep.

FORTY-SEVEN

Natalie

I sit at my desk, looking through the photographs I printed out. There is no mistaking Lucas and Haley in these high-quality images, yet I hesitate to show them to Andrea with the newfound information. If I go forward with this, I may be putting myself and Emma in danger. I continue to stare at the photos. I need to do this.

Haley's out sick again today, and I wonder if she's having second thoughts about her late-night meeting with Lucas on the playground. At least I know she's not pregnant.

I continue to stare at the pictures for a few more minutes, then place them back into the manilla envelope. I have about ten minutes until I need to go down to Lucas's classroom. I think about it a few more minutes and decide I'm going to wait until the end of the day after bus duty. Then I'll show Andrea the pictures and see how this all plays out. Now I need to go down to his classroom and get this part of the day over with. I dread seeing him.

My high-heeled boots click on the hard vinyl hallway

flooring as I travel down to my destination. I take a deep breath and grasp the doorknob. There's a change in the air almost as soon as I enter the room. Lucas stands at the front of the classroom speaking about the new chapter that the class will be starting today. He acknowledges me with a brief look that swirls with hostility and something else that I can't quite pinpoint.

I stand by Heather's desk and stare at him as he talks about line segments and hope the time passes quickly. I think of Haley and make a mental note to text her tonight and check in with her. She's been out sick for two days. Did something more happen that night she met Lucas on the playground?

"Okay, class, get out your iPads; you're going to do some practice with line segments on there to see what you remember and then we'll know what areas we need to focus on," Lucas says, his gaze intent on me. "Put your earbuds in, or if you don't have any there are headphones in the basket on the front table."

The room hums with low chatter and desks opening and closing as students retrieve their iPads. He continues to stand at the front of the room until everyone has their earbuds in or headphones on.

Lucas walks to me and says in a quiet, tense voice, "May I speak to you at my desk?"

I nod and we walk back to his desk at the back of the room, out of earshot of the students now working on their iPads.

We stand by his desk now, his familiar woodsy cologne surrounding me at this close distance. His dark eyes bore into me. He moves even closer to me, uncomfortably so, but I don't back away. "Natalie, sweet Natalie," he says in a voice barely above a whisper. "It's been a few years."

"Yes, Lucas, it has," I reply. His breath is hot against my neck. He *does* recognize me.

His lips curve into a smile. "I couldn't figure it out, why you were so cold toward me and this obsession you have with my wife; all of it was so strange, but now it makes sense."

"Really? When did you have this realization?"

"Olivia was talking about you *again* this morning." He hisses this, barely an inch from my ear. "And that's when I really thought about it, thought about you and how you inserted yourself into my wife's life. There was always something familiar about you, but I couldn't place it, especially that day when you were lingering by my desk. I remember having a weird feeling about you that day, that we'd met before. Then everything fell together. I know who you are. I can't believe I didn't remember you earlier, but it's been twenty years." He looks me up and down with a sneer. "And you've changed a fair bit."

"Only this morning?" I ask, thinking about the note in Emma's backpack the other day. My heart rate increases and heat rises in my body.

"Yes." He moves even closer to me, his voice still barely a whisper now so the students can't hear. "Then of course I realized the reason for your behavior. So cold to me, so interested in Olivia. I don't know why I didn't see it before; I should have known. Simple jealousy, Olivia has what you always wanted." He pauses, grinning cockily, so sure of himself. "Me. You always wanted me. I remember how you used to call me nonstop."

Fury floods through my body now, pure anger; the nerve of this man and his inflated ego infuriates me. I stomp my heeled boot promptly on top of his dress shoe, and he winces. I hold it there.

"I was calling you because I was *pregnant* with your baby," I hiss back as I grind my heel, enjoying his squirm. "You're the last thing I'd ever want."

He glares at me.

"And I knew I was right about Haley," I say, lifting my boot from his foot. I slam it down on his foot again, and again he winces. "And Olivia knows too. And soon, so will Andrea."

I walk away to check on my students.

. . .

I grab the manilla envelope from inside my school bag and stalk up to Andrea's office after bus duty. I round the corner, but the lights are off in the office.

"Sorry, Natalie, Andrea's gone for the day," Mindy calls from the front desk. "She had a doctor appointment."

"Oh," I say, disappointment filling me. I should have done this earlier; now it has to wait another day. I grip the envelope. "Okay, thanks, Mindy."

I walk back to my classroom, place the manilla envelope back into my bag, and sigh, standing in the quiet for a few minutes, thinking about everything that happened over the past week. I want everything to be over. I want a normal peaceful life. I grab my bag and the rest of my stuff, then head down to the walker door to get Emma and go home. I only want to eat dinner and lie down on the sofa to rest; I'm exhausted.

I trudge down the hall, murmuring goodbyes to those who wish me the same, and finally reach the walker door, now a headache forming, and I cannot wait to get home to take something for it. The walker door is open, but Mrs. Stamos isn't standing by it; instead, a substitute stands there.

"Oh, hello," I say to her. "Are you in for Mrs. Stamos?"

"Yes." She nods.

I smile and continue out the door and look to the right where Emma always waits by the brick wall with her friend Becky.

She isn't there.

Nobody stands by the brick wall.

"Where's Emma?" I ask the sub. "Where's my daughter?"

"What?"

"Two girls, kindergarteners, always wait by that brick wall." I point to the wall. "Emma and Becky. They wait for me. Becky walks home with her sister, and Emma goes with me."

"Um... there were two girls standing by the wall earlier, but they were picked up, I suppose, or walked home."

My heart drops. This is it, my worst nightmare come true. I try to keep my voice even; maybe Becky's mom took her home, for a playdate. "Who picked them up? Did they take both girls or just Emma?"

The woman wears a confused look. "I really don't know. They were there for a few minutes and then they were gone. I was helping another student who dumped his backpack and there were papers everywhere. I'm sorry, I don't know..."

My mind spins. Where is Emma?

Lucas.

It has to be him.

"Was there a male teacher down here? Maybe she went back into the school?" I ask the substitute.

"Oh my goodness, I'm so sorry. I don't know. When I was helping that boy, I stepped away from the door. I guess it's possible," she stammers; she looks terrified.

It had to be him. He's trying to get back at me for this afternoon.

He's taken Emma. Fear shoots through me, mixed with an overwhelming anger.

What if he hurts her? He has a violent side I didn't know about.

He *killed* that girl!

My body shakes and tears sting my eyes, but I don't have time for that.

He is not going to get away with this!

I turn around and run back into the school. I race down the hall to his classroom and fling open the door, a loud clang as it hits the wall, then it slams shut. Lucas sits at his desk, pristinely organized, right down to the small round container of multicolored paper clips sitting on the front of the desk. He looks up, a smile on his face, which quickly fades when he sees me.

"Where is she?" I demand, stomping over to his desk. "Tell me where she is now, you stupid ass!"

He feigns surprise. "What? Who?"

I stand across from his desk. "Emma, my daughter!"

He leans back in his chair. "Oh, right. I believe she's in kindergarten."

I take my hand and swipe it across his desk, and everything flies onto the floor, crashing into a loud heap. Lucas jumps up, the desk chair slamming into the file cabinets behind him.

"What the fuck!" he yells.

I unzip my school bag and pull out the manilla envelope and show him the pictures of him and Haley on the sliding board.

"You better tell me right now where she is!" I bellow. "Or these will be plastered all over school. Stop messing around with me and tell me where Emma is, right now!"

"How did you get those?" he demands.

"I followed you!"

"You are a stalker. You are obsessed with me!"

"You're obsessed with yourself!" I yell back. He tries to move close to me. I round the back table. "You're not going to get away with this. There's still lots of people in the school. I'm surprised someone hasn't come in here yet. They will if we keep yelling."

He stops for a moment.

"Now show me where she is," I tell him.

He smiles and puts his hands up. "I'll show you, then you'll give me those pictures."

I'll agree to anything; Emma is all that matters. I wave him to the door. "Let's go."

We walk silently down the semi-empty hall, and I'm careful to keep my distance from him, then turn left, walking straight toward the gym. Lucas opens the door, and we walk inside, the door slamming shut with a loud thud. Now we stand in the empty gymnasium.

Only one light is on at the right side of the gym, and a dim light shines from behind the red stage curtain located on the far left. Lucas turns left and walks toward the stage.

"Over here," he says as I trail along.

We travel up three steps and walk onto the stage going behind the heavy red curtain to the space with subdued lighting behind it. Chairs are still set up from the band concert last week, creating eerie shadows along the back wall.

Lucas stands off to the side, his legs apart, his arms crossed. "Give me the pictures, Natalie."

He points to a large door at the side of the stage. Splatters of red and white paint adorn the front. "She's in there."

I run over and yank the door open, but it's empty inside. He is instantly behind me, shoving me inside the space. I elbow him in the eye, and he cries out, but keeps coming at me. He tries to grab the envelope, but I hold it close to my chest. He gives me a hard shove and slams the door shut.

"Let me out!" I yell and pound on the door.

"Give me those pictures!"

"Where is my daughter?"

The closet is so dark without any hint of light and smells like bleach, so my guess is that cleaning supplies are stored in here. Silence is the only sound in this space. Then music starts to play; the band must have after-school rehearsals in the music room. I push on the door again, but it doesn't budge. If I yell loud enough, someone should hear me. Precious minutes are slipping away. I need to find Emma.

"Lucas, open this door!" I scream. "Now!"

"Slide the pictures under the door," he instructs. "Then I'll tell you where your daughter is."

I fumble with the envelope, tears stinging my eyes, bend down, and slide it under the heavy door. Why is he doing this?

What if he doesn't let me out? Fear snakes through me realizing Emma may be in serious danger.

Lucas quickly snatches it up.

The door opens.

"Where is she?" I demand.

He shrugs. "I don't know. I didn't take her."

I run at him, hitting him with a balled fist straight in the chest, but he barely flinches. "You're lying! You monster!"

He shrugs again. "I'm not. I don't know where your daughter is. I just wanted the pictures." He moves closer to me, pushing me onto the floor of the closet. "Delete them and destroy any other copies you have or you'll be sorry. This is me being nice, Natalie. You've never seen me angry. Trust me, that's something you don't want to see."

I scramble back, trying to gain my footing. "Don't threaten me!"

He pushes me hard against the back of the closet and I sink to the floor. "I'm serious," he says, towering over me. "Don't cross me."

I reach out my hand to grab a spray bottle of cleaning liquid sitting next to me on the floor and squeeze.

"Argh!" he yelps, jumping away from me, his hand trying to shield his eyes.

I jump to my feet and don't waste another moment on him. I race out of the closet, down the steps, and run out of the school. I quickly cross the street to our house, hoping Emma may be there. *Please let her be there. Please.*

I'm out of breath by the time I reach our front door. My sides are hurting and I can barely breathe. I stop for a moment to catch my breath and notice the front door is slightly ajar. I hear movement inside.

"Emma!" I call, rushing inside.

I stop dead in my tracks.

A person sits at my kitchen table, wearing a black T-shirt

and faded jeans, while drinking a soda, likely taken from my refrigerator. A bag of nacho chips sits on the table in front of him.

A ghost from the past.

"Hello, Natalie," he says.

My heart is pounding so loudly and not from my frantic run across the street. Sweat trickles down my back and the shackles of fear grab hold of me. My worst nightmare is sitting in my kitchen.

Theo.

FORTY-EIGHT

Natalie

"Why are you here?" I hate how my voice sounds. Weak. Timid. Scared.

He smiles, taking another sip of soda, enjoying my panic as he always did. Sickness snakes through my entire body, and I fear I may throw up, but must push it aside. I must find Emma! Be strong, don't show that you're scared of him, even though he must know it. He always liked when I was scared. It always made things worse. Where could he have taken Emma? My stomach flips again.

Time has not been kind to Theo. It's only been six years, but he looks like he's aged at least ten. The scar above his right eyebrow is still there, now joined by another longer scar on his left cheek. His skin is sallow, and a few wrinkles are visible, his hair thinning. He's much more muscular now; his arms ripple under the form-fitting shirt, but his eyes, more yellowish than I remember, are the same, cunning, and sharp, ready to strike at me any moment.

"You know why. Actually..." He pauses. "I've been here for a while. This is just the first time I let you see me."

I stare at him. "You were the one sneaking around." My voice is getting stronger now.

"That was me. It was kind of fun, seeing you get so freaked out. Watching you sleep in your bed." His voice deepens. "I've really enjoyed playing secret stranger with you."

Fear grabs me, but I don't want to let him know he still terrifies me.

"Why aren't you in jail?"

"Oh, yeah, jail." He stands now, a sneer across his face. "The place you sent me to when you lied."

He moves closer to me, looking me up and down. "You still look pretty good, Nat. Real good."

I stare at him. "Where's Emma?"

He laughs. "Emma? Oh, you mean our daughter?"

"*My* daughter!"

He pushes me against the wall and slams the front door shut. His hands are on my neck, and he grazes the side of my cheek with his wet lips. He smells like nacho cheese chips and sweat. Maybe the sweat is me.

"Don't you miss this," he whispers, his tongue now licking my face. I feel remnants of the nacho chips hanging on my cheek. His hands grab my breasts, and he squeezes hard. "I do."

"No!" I summon all my strength and push him off me.

"Oh, so you still want to play games." He laughs. "That's okay, I like games."

I run to the living room, grab a vase from the side table, and hurl it at him.

He ducks and lunges at me. He pushes me to the floor and we roll around on the carpet. He grabs my hair and pulls it back roughly until my neck aches.

"Please, Theo, don't..." I plead. "What do you want? I'll do anything to get Emma back."

Surprisingly, he stops and lets go of me, thoughtful for a moment. "She's a cool kid."

Then he laughs again.

"Okay, so it's going to be all business with you. You'll be happy to know all the charges were dropped; there was new proof in the case. I'm a free man and I have some business with you."

"What business?"

"Where's my money, Nat?"

"It's upstairs," I say. "I'll get it for you. Then you'll tell me where Emma is."

"I already looked through your closets and through your bedroom," he says. "It's not there."

"It is." I hurry upstairs. "I'll show you."

I run to my bedroom and dive into my closet: Under a stack of sweaters inside an old backpack, wrapped in a Target plastic bag, is where I last hid the small leather bag containing the cash. I unzip the backpack and shove my hand inside.

The bag is empty.

My mind blanks.

Fuck.

I stand up, dropping the backpack. Theo stands behind me. He grabs me by the arms and throws me against the wall. My head hits a framed photo hanging on the wall and it falls, glass shattering on the floor.

"I told you it wasn't there!" he yells.

I turn around. He slaps me across the face.

"I want the money. You took everything from me. You didn't even tell me I have a daughter!"

My face stings from the slap as my mind scrambles for an answer.

"No, I know, I was wrong. I should have told you."

"Yeah, yah think?" Theo twirls around and does a little dance. "Oh, honey, we have a child. It's a girl!"

I smile nervously. He's crazier than I remember.

"Yes, of course," I say. "And I do know where the money is."

He pushes me into the wall. "Stop dicking me around."

I shake my head, my mind scrambling for something to distract him. "I'm sorry, I can't trick you. This guy I know, uh, Lucas, has it. I'm friends with his wife. He stole it from me. From you. He stole your money."

"You're lying." He stares at me. "You're a liar."

"I'm not," I insist as he squeezes my arms until they redden.

"Then we're going there," he says, letting go of my arms. "And we'll get my money or we'll find out you're a liar. Again."

"I'm not lying. There is a guy named Lucas and it's all true. I know it's so crazy, but it's real. I want Emma back," I plead. "I won't lie to you again."

Theo throws his head back and laughs. "That's rich. You won't lie to me."

He paces the room for a time, then grabs my arm, dragging me along with him. "You're taking me to this Lucas guy."

* * *

Ten minutes later, we arrive at Lucas and Olivia's pretty Cape Cod-style home. Lucas has clearly not been home long; he stands in the doorway, facing Olivia, who also stands in the doorway. They're yelling at each other.

"You lock the garage door and now you tell me I can't come into *my* house!" Lucas fumes. "Who the hell do you think you are?"

"Well, I'm not a murderer!" Olivia yells back. "You killed that girl in Pittsburgh."

"I did no such thing!"

"Say her name." Olivia stares him down. "Her name was Angie and you stabbed her to death!"

THE INNOCENT WIFE   239

"You crazy bitch." Lucas loses any shred of composure and punches the open front door, right beside Olivia.

Olivia doesn't stop. She pulls a necklace from her pocket and shoves it in his face. "This necklace is proof. I found it inside your safe. This is Angie's necklace. You gave it to her!"

Lucas stares at the necklace but doesn't say anything.

"You followed her to Billy's Bar that night and you killed her."

Lucas still wears the same clothes from school, but his hair is tousled and messy. His eyes are red from the cleaning liquid I sprayed in them earlier. Anger and confusion cover his face as he argues with Olivia, then alarm as he turns to see me and Theo marching up his sidewalk.

"What the hell?" he demands as Theo pushes past me and shoves Lucas on his way inside the house. Olivia quickly jumps back. I follow. Theo grabs Lucas by the shirt, getting in his face. "Billy's Bar in Pittsburgh?"

"Yes, he killed a girl named Angie at that bar," Olivia offers.

Theo's eyes glaze over when she says the words, and he smashes his head into Lucas's. "*You're* the asshole who killed that girl? And you stole my fucking money?"

Lucas shoves him back. "I didn't kill anyone. What money? I didn't do anything." He turns to me. "You brought this thug to beat me up? I told you, I don't know where your daughter is!"

"I rotted away in a jail cell because of you for years!" Theo punches Lucas in the face, knocking him down. "All of you, all of you are liars!"

Lucas scrambles to his feet and punches Theo, who trips and lands on the floor. Lucas looks at me. "Who is this guy? I don't have Emma or any money. I don't know anything!"

"You killed that girl in Pittsburgh," Theo yells, jumping up and now is in Lucas's face. "And I went to jail for it!"

Lucas freezes.

Theo's eyes darken to a cold black. "I lost my entire life

because of you," he howls. "You're going to die now, *motherfucker*." And he punches Lucas in the face.

The two men trade punches in the foyer of the house. Olivia is now standing at the top of the stairs, and I'm still standing at the front door, both of us immobile at the moment as we watch them fight.

"I'm going to kill you!" Theo yells, grabbing Lucas again. He throws him into the dining room to the right directly into the china cabinet, breaking the glass panels. Glass shatters all around them onto the floor.

Lucas punches Theo and he flies over the dining table. Theo jumps up, grabs the ceramic vase from the center of the table, filled with yellow flowers, and breaks it over Lucas's head. The two men grab each other and wrestle each other to the floor, trading punches, blood and one tooth flying in the air. Lucas punches him again, pushing Theo into the front window. Theo grabs the curtains to stabilize himself, pulling them down to the floor in a loud crash.

I stare, hovering by the stairs, unsure of what to do. I need to find Emma and I need Theo to do that. I don't have my phone; it's still in my bag at school. *What should I do?*

There is a crash as Lucas jumps up and tips over the china cabinet, its contents spilling to the floor, plates, saucers, and cups crashing into a pile, and blocking Theo from him, momentarily. For a moment the room is silent, eerily so, then Theo throws his head back and cackles like a madman. A maniacal look fills his eyes as he stares at Lucas, who's trying to round the dining table on the other end of the fallen cabinet.

"You're out of your league, pretty boy," Theo growls, then lunges forward.

He jumps up on the table and tackles Lucas, landing on top of him, pounding his fists into his head, his face, every part of him. Blood covers Lucas's face, his nose clearly broken, and he's not fighting back anymore.

He's not moving.

I glance up the stairway to see Olivia still on the stairs. She holds her cell phone up to show 911 on the line. Minutes pass, agonizingly slow, then the police show up a few seconds later, bursting through the already open front door, guns blazing.

Theo is still pounding on Lucas, seemingly enjoying it. Blood, his and Lucas's, covers him and his clothes; his front tooth is missing as he continues to laugh. The police arrest him and handcuff him.

I run to him, this psychopathic lunatic, the biological father of my daughter. "Where is Emma? Tell me!"

Theo stares at me, blood pouring from his mouth from the missing tooth, then starts laughing. "I don't know."

I tell the police that my daughter is missing, and they put an Amber Alert out on her, but Theo insists he doesn't know anything. I know he has her hidden somewhere; I have to find her, but I don't know what to do next.

Olivia and I hold each other as the police take Theo away and the coroner comes to take Lucas. He is pronounced dead at 5:15 p.m., only an hour since he locked me in the closet behind the stage. The news leaves me numb; the only thing I can feel is fear for Emma.

"We have to find her," I cry. "Where could he have taken her? Why would she go with him? She wouldn't go with a stranger."

"I may have the answer," Olivia says, placing something in my hand.

FORTY-NINE

Olivia

Once the police arrive, everything happens in a blur. They take Theo away. Natalie is consumed with worry about Emma. I walk over to where Lucas lies on the floor as paramedics attend to him. None of this seems real. I'm walking around as if in a dream.

A nightmare.

"No, madam," the young paramedic says. "You shouldn't see him like this. I'm sorry, but he is deceased."

"He is?" My question sounds hollow. I do see him before they cover him with a white sheet. His handsome face now disfigured by a broken nose, possibly a broken jaw, and blood, so much blood.

He's gone.

Dead.

Lucas wasn't a good person. He lied to me and so many others. He killed that girl. I know he did, and he cheated on me. But he had good qualities too, and I loved him for many years before realizing his true nature. I don't wish him dead. Certainly not like this.

I sit on a dining chair staring at him covered by a white sheet waiting for the coroner's arrival. Life can change in an instant. This is immediate proof. I've felt like I've been in a standstill in my life for so long and now change is flooding through like a tidal wave, overwhelming me, but I'm determined to withstand its fury. I watch the coroner declare his time of death, watch them put Lucas into a long, dark bag and zip it up, then carry him away. I never knew what happens when someone dies; I don't know if I ever thought about it before all of this. They told me not to, but I had to see him leaving our house, knowing he will never return. He will never know the baby I carry inside my body. Tears fall from my eyes.

Something catches my eye under the china cabinet next to the space where my husband lay only moments earlier.

A cell phone.

Theo's phone.

FIFTY

Natalie

I take the phone Olivia hands me; drops of blood are splattered on the cracked screen.

"I think it's Theo's," she says. "It was lying on the floor next to Lucas."

Luckily, no security code is needed, and I quickly look at his recent texts. The name at the top of the list stuns me. How would he know her?

Candace.

Jake's wife? No, it can't be her.

I click on it. The last text is Theo asking Candace to pick Emma up at school and that he's going to finally "catch up" with Natalie. Also to tell Emma that Dad loves her.

Dad?

I remember how Emma would sometimes use Dad instead of Daddy, but I always thought she meant Jake. And her insistence that "Dad" had gotten her that Barbie left on our front porch.

Dad is Theo.

He's met Emma, spent time with her. Candace has arranged it! I knew something was wrong with her. I'm going to fucking *kill* her.

How could she do this? What is wrong with her? She put my baby in danger!

Anger pulses through me so strongly, my head pounds and I think I may throw up, again. How dare she do this? I'm certain Jake doesn't know; he would never allow it. So, she must be hiding it from him too. How does she know Theo? How did she get into contact with him? How could she possibly know him?

"We have to go to Jake's house right now!" I say to Olivia, showing her the texts. "I think Emma's there."

"What the hell?" Olivia asks, reading the texts. "Let's go."

We hurry out to her car and drive over to Jake and Candace's house. When we arrive, Olivia parks the car and I race to the front door and fling it open.

Emma sits on the floor in the living room playing with her Barbie Dreamhouse and rearranging the furniture in the pink bedroom. The tension in my body calms slightly. *Thank God she's okay.* I run to her and pick her up, hugging her tightly.

"Oh, I love you so much," I gush. "I'm so happy to see you!"

She giggles. "Mommy, you're squishing me!"

I give her a bunch of kisses, and she laughs more.

Jake walks in, a surprised look on his face. "Oh, Nat, I was just going to call you. Candace said she picked Emma up today, but I didn't think we had her today."

I give Emma another hug and look at her. "It's so nice outside. Why don't you take your Barbies onto your swing set?"

"Okay, they will like that," Emma agrees, grabbing two dolls and hurrying out the sliding glass door in the kitchen and out to the backyard.

"Where's Candace?" I demand; my voice growls.

Jake's surprise turns to concern. "What's wrong? What's going on?"

"Candace has been in touch with Theo. She's been allowing him to spend time with Emma, and she picked Emma up at school today so he could come see me!" I yell. "She let our daughter spend time with that psycho!"

"What? She did what!" Jake is dumbfounded. "Are you okay; did he hurt you?"

"I'm okay, especially now that I know Emma is safe."

"Where's he now?" Jake asks.

"Back in jail," I say. "He killed Lucas."

"What?" Jake shouts. "Candace!"

"He thought I had something of his and he wouldn't tell me where Emma was, so I said Lucas had it and we went to his house. They got into a violent fight."

"Fucking crazy. And Candace contacted Theo? How? Why? I don't understand any of this." Jake paces around the room. "I told her his name once when she asked, and that he's in jail. Really that's it. I never went into detail, just that he was dangerous. I would never put you or Emma in danger, you have to know that."

"I do, Jake, this was all Candace," I say. "I don't know how, or why."

"We're going to find out." Jake's jaw sets firmly, as it does when he gets angry. "I don't understand any of this."

Candace finally joins us in the living room. She stares at us.

"It's not right that Emma doesn't know her real father," she says.

Jake's eyes darken. "I'm her real father!"

"You are and you're wonderful," she replies, softening when she looks at him. Then she turns to me with an icy glare. "But Theo should know about Emma. He is so good with her."

I lunge at her, but Jake holds me back.

Candace scoffs. "Please, Natalie, you were so offended when I wanted Emma to call me mom, but you didn't even tell her about her real father!"

"Shut up, Candace!" I yell. "Jake is the only father Emma will ever have. How did you get in touch with Theo?"

Candace smiles. "Theo is my cousin; I couldn't believe it when Jake told me his name, but suddenly it all made sense. He's innocent of that girl's murder and you know it."

I stare at her. "How can you believe that? Did he tell you how he abused me and how he's a criminal? He's a fucking lunatic and you allowed him to be around Emma! Did he tell you he was breaking into our house and sneaking around too? What if he would have hurt Emma? How could you do this?"

Jake is standing between us looking like a deer caught in the headlights. As angry as I am at Candace, I remind myself the only important fact is that Emma is safe. Theo is in jail and can't hurt us. Jake has to sort out his marriage, but I can promise Candace will never be around Emma again.

"Theo is not all bad!" Candace insists. "And he wouldn't even be in jail if it wasn't for you. He deserves to know his daughter."

I stare at her and realize it's pointless to argue with someone who has that logic about Theo. He's poison. He'll always be poison and I'll not allow my daughter to be around him.

Ever.

End of discussion.

"I'm taking Emma home," I say, brushing past Candace as I go out to the backyard to get my daughter.

Emma and I hurry out to the car where Olivia waits for us. Leaving Jake to sort out his marriage.

FIFTY-ONE

Olivia

Lucas's funeral is well attended and although I do mourn the man I thought he was at some point, I tire of the many people from school going on about him being a pillar of the community and how charming and wonderful he was. A real life of the party.

Well, the party's over. My new party is just beginning.

I met Natalie's gaze many times when I was deluged with mourners. She's the only one who understands. She knows all of Lucas's secrets and mine. Nothing is hidden between us. We told police that we thought Theo, Natalie's abusive ex, had kidnapped Emma and then he took Natalie to my house to confront Lucas about some business he had with him. Theo walked in and the two men started arguing and fighting and Theo killed Lucas. We didn't know what the business was about; even though Theo ranted about Lucas killing the girl in Pittsburgh, nobody believed him, or cared, I guess. Candace didn't come forward to the police with her story about Natalie lying under oath, surprisingly. Although, I suppose she could have been charged with stalking Natalie, and she didn't have any proof, only Theo's word, a convicted murderer, against Natalie's, so that's probably why she kept quiet. At least Theo will be locked up for a long time; I know Natalie is relieved with that information.

Finally, the crowd thins a bit and I step away to use the restroom. Natalie follows me inside and Haley is with her. Natalie locks the door and checks under the stalls to see if we're alone. We are.

"Olivia," Haley says. "I asked Natalie if I could talk privately with both of you."

"Oh, okay," I reply.

"I want to apologize to you. I talked to Natalie about it, and she thought I should talk to you. I was seeing Lucas, but it was just kissing and making out, that's it, and I'm so embarrassed about it. I don't know what I was thinking doing that with a married man and I didn't feel right about it at all. I promised myself it wouldn't happen again, but then his death... I'm so sorry about everything and I hope you can forgive me one day. I was so disrespectful to you."

I smile at her. "I know he lied to you to get you to trust him; he's done that in the past. I forgive you and I hope you will keep all of this between us."

Haley nods. "I'm not talking about it ever again once we leave this bathroom."

"Perfect," Natalie says.

Haley turns to Natalie. "And Natalie, thank you for letting me help in your classroom. I've learned so much from you."

Natalie smiles. "And I thought you thought I was a bit strange."

"Well... there were a few times," Haley replies with a grin.

"Okay," I say. "Everything is good between the three of us."

"Yes," the other two women say in unison.

. . .

I'm the last one standing at the burial site, perching on the uncomfortable folding chair and staring at the dark blue coffin containing Lucas's body that will soon be lowered into the ground by the two burly men who now stand with the funeral director waiting for me to say my final goodbye. This is more difficult than I expected; I spent so much of my life, my entire adult life, with this man and even though he wasn't the best, I still mourn him and feel a bit lost about being on my own. I don't think that makes me weak, but my life will be dramatically different without him. I was so dependent on him and now I realize I didn't need to be, yet it took me years to realize this fact. The mind and thinking patterns are such powerful influences on our lives, both in keeping us in the same place as well as moving us forward.

I grip the red rose I took from the funeral spray on the top of the casket and think about the first time Lucas got me a dozen red roses for my seventeenth birthday. Even after all that happened and how Lucas treated me and others, a small part of me still loves him and probably always will.

I stand up and place the rose on top of the coffin.

Goodbye, Lucas.

FIFTY-TWO

Natalie

Olivia stays overnight at my house after the funeral. It has been a strange day with everyone going on about Lucas's warm personality, how everyone liked him, and how he was a pillar of the Peyton Heights School community. Olivia and I shared several glances throughout the service. We are the only two people who know all his real truths. But the truth is that Lucas wasn't completely bad—is anyone? A bad person or a good person, statements in the simplest of terms, because everyone has shades of good and bad; aren't we all merely shades of gray, only some shades are much darker. Very few know all the facets of another's personality, but Olivia and I know all of Lucas's sides.

But now he's gone, and Theo is back in jail, hopefully for the rest of his life. I certainly never want to see that lunatic again, although Olivia and I will have to testify at his court hearing eventually. Olivia and I can continue our lives without threats or intimidation from either one. I made Olivia a hot cup of tea and sent her to bed; she'd sleep in my room, and I'd sleep with Emma. Olivia looked so exhausted by the day's events, and I hope a good night's sleep will restore her energy. It's just after nine when I go upstairs to check on them. Both Olivia and Emma lost in peaceful slumber, and I tiptoe back downstairs.

I spoke to Jake briefly yesterday and things are not going well between him and Candace. He couldn't tolerate her dishonesty and how she put Emma in danger by spending time with Theo, a known criminal. Seems like divorce is on the cards for those two.

Jake's right, honesty is almost always the right choice.

But there are a few rare exceptions.

I walk over to a large wicker basket by the side of the sofa. Nestled under a few blankets, I pull out the object I seek.

A small leather bag.

Full of cash.

The night after everything happened with Theo and Lucas, Emma and I were getting ready for bed. I'd completely forgotten about the bag after the day's events. I went into the bathroom to brush my teeth when Emma said she forgot something in her backpack. When I came out of the bathroom, she was playing on the floor in her bedroom. The leather bag sat to the side and stacks of cash surrounded her. Theo's money, my money now.

"I'm playing bank," she announced.

She had found the bag in my closet and had it in her backpack the entire time. I asked her if I could play too, and she said yes because she was tired. She told me the money got her hands dirty, showing me the black smudges on them. We hurried to the bathroom to wash them, then she got into her bed, and I gathered the cash, put it back into the bag, zipped it shut, and brought it down to the living room, hiding it in the blankets.

I'm going to need a better hiding place...

EPILOGUE
ONE YEAR LATER

Natalie

The warm May sun shines down on us as we find a few empty folding chairs at the back of the outdoor graduation ceremony. It's a busy affair, and we are lucky to find these seats for this special event. We settle in and I look at the rows of people sitting in front of us, and beyond them to the stage, decorated in bright red and white balloons, the school's colors.

Emma wiggles in her chair. "When will it start, Mom?" she asks. She wears her new purple sundress and a cute white sweater with purple polka dots. She looks so cute and so grown up at six years old.

"Soon," I reply. I place my left hand on top of my right; a flash of the beautiful gem on it always surprises me, even though I've worn it for almost two months now.

I stare at it. A stunning princess cut diamond that sparkles and shines and makes me smile every time I look at it. Another hand intertwines with mine and that makes me smile even more.

"Still love looking at that ring?" Ryan asks. "You're not having second thoughts, are you?"

I smile at my fiancé. "No second thoughts. I love being engaged to you."

Ryan grins. He leans over and kisses me. "I love you."

I return his kiss and squeeze his hand. He makes me feel so loved and special. He's the partner I've been looking for all my life.

About two months after everything happened with Theo and Lucas, Ryan and I started dating and everything about the relationship was real. Feelings, connection, trust, love. Unlike any relationship I'd ever experienced and now, we've been engaged for two months and planning our wedding for next spring. The happiness I feel with him is unreal to me; I never thought I'd have a relationship like this, I love him so much.

"Oh, you two," Jake teases, sitting on the other side of Emma.

"They're in love," Emma whispers, giggling.

"Yes, they are." Jake laughs.

"Are you and Olivia in love?" Emma asks.

I look at Jake, and Olivia sitting next to him. They are holding hands. Maybe not in love yet, but well under way. Six months ago, Jake's second divorce was final, and he and Olivia became close friends. Last month they announced they were dating. The way they looked at each other gave me such joy. So much love and adoration that both deserve so much.

"We like each other very much," Olivia says, smiling at Jake.

"Very much," he replies, meeting her gaze.

A baby's cry distracts them. Olivia stands and lifts Isabella from the stroller, soothing her, and in a few minutes, she falls back to sleep, but Olivia keeps her in her arms. She is an amazing woman. After everything that has happened, she seems to grow stronger every single day. She's taking a few college classes online too, and she thinks she would like to become a teacher eventually, but she's taking it slow, step by step. New motherhood and going to college are a lot to tackle at one time. I'm so lucky to have her as my friend.

The ceremony is beginning now. As the graduates are called, young individuals cross the stage to collect their diploma, dressed in their graduation gowns in the bright school colors. Haley strides across the stage, her dark hair gleaming and her smile even brighter as she accepts her high school diploma.

I'm so proud of her. She asked us to be here today. In the fall she starts college for her teaching degree, on a full scholarship. She has excellent grades and with my help we found a lot of opportunities for her. I can't wait to see where life takes her; I'm sure she has a bright future ahead of her.

Ryan squeezes my hand again and I squeeze back. So many new beginnings for all of us.

Olivia

I cuddle Isabella and look up to see Jake staring at us. Jake, kind, loving, supportive Jake, who has been such a support to me over these last several months, and I have tried to be the same for him as he dealt with his divorce being finalized from Candace.

What a different type of man than Lucas, in all the right ways. I know that we've only dated for a month, but I feel like I can tell him anything and he will be right by my side.

An equal partner in everything.

I'm probably getting a bit ahead of myself, but I'm completely myself around Jake. I'm not ever changing or agreeing to something just because someone else wants it. It's such a freeing feeling, and Jake and I have so much fun together, just being with one another. I'm excited to see where our relationship leads in the future.

My gaze moves to Natalie, my best friend. How strange that

it was Lucas who brought us together and that this bond developed between us; I felt that connection with her the first day we met in the cafeteria, although I didn't understand it at the time. My heart floods with joy seeing her sitting with Ryan, staring at the gorgeous engagement ring on her finger. She's the happiest I've ever seen her; Jake says the same and he's known her much longer than me, and I feel both of us are traveling down a road of sunshine and happiness, leaving the darkness and gloom of our pasts behind us.

Haley accepts her diploma, and I fill with pride and excitement for her and the next chapter of her life. Isabella wiggles in my arms and I hold her close to my body until she settles. I smell her sweet head, lavender scented from her baby shampoo, and think about how lucky she is to have so many strong women in her life.

And I am one of them.

A LETTER FROM THE AUTHOR

Huge thanks for reading *The Innocent Wife*. I hope you enjoyed this intense and emotional domestic thriller as Natalie and Olivia navigate their troubled lives. If you want to join other readers in hearing all about my new releases and bonus content, you can sign up for my newsletter.

www.stormpublishing.co/sally-royer-derr

If you enjoyed this book and could spare a few moments to leave a review that would be hugely appreciated. Even a short review can make all the difference in encouraging a reader to discover my books for the first time. Thank you so much.

The Innocent Wife was such a fun story for me to write since it took place in a school setting, and I worked in special education for many years. While this story certainly has many twists and turns, I think the most powerful aspect is the friendship between Natalie and Olivia as each deal with past traumas and find strength in one another.

Thanks again for being part of this amazing journey with me and I hope you'll stay in touch—I have so many more stories and ideas to entertain you with!

Sally

www.sallyroyer-derr.com

KEEP IN TOUCH WITH THE AUTHOR

www.sallyroyer-derr.com

- facebook.com/SallyRoyerDerrAuthorPage
- x.com/sallyroyerderr
- instagram.com/srderr
- bookbub.com/profile/sally-royer-derr
- tiktok.com/@sallyroyerderr

ACKNOWLEDGEMENTS

A warm thank you to my incredibly brilliant editor, Emily Gowers, who takes my first draft and works with me to take my writing to another level. It's so much fun working with you to create these wild, twisty books! Also, huge thanks to Oliver Rhodes and the entire amazing team at Storm Publishing, who are always there to support my books in all stages of production.

All my love to my handsome and thoughtful husband, Mike, who always believed and supported my dream of being an author. I'm so happy you've been by my side as my partner in crime for so many years, and look forward to many, many more!

To my Penn-Bernville friends, this book is entirely fictional, but the settings in my mind are the hallways and classrooms I've worked in for many years with you. Thanks for the good memories.

Thank you to my FABULOUS readers!

Thank you, thank you, thank you, my amazing readers! Please keep reading, writing reviews, and talking about my books. Your excitement for my stories inspires me to write more for you to enjoy!

Printed in Great Britain
by Amazon